A Misted Mirror

Gillian Jones

Gillian Jones wrote **A MISTED MIRROR** as a response to her late husband, Keith Jones's illness with Parkinson's Disease and to his poetry. Structured around the poetry, the novel imagines and explores the life together of a fictional couple, Sarah and David, with flashbacks to before they met, and chronicles David's later decline with Parkinson's Disease and dementia. Early readers have found it a powerful and compelling story, of a young man sowing wild oats in Africa, confronting his demons in the hothouse of a London arts community, and finding pleasure and satisfaction in a second marriage, family and career. The results of his illness come as a heart-rending contrast but mitigated by a generous late-flowering of his poetry.

After graduating from St Andrews University, **GILLIAN JONES** worked as a teacher in many parts of the world, including Spain, Portugal, and Colombia. Later, after specialist training in Teaching English as a Foreign Language, she was sent by the British Council as an ELT expert to Teheran where she met and married her husband. On returning to the United Kingdom she spent three years as a writer and producer in television. Gillian has two sons and now lives in the South of England.

Proverse Prize Joint-Winner 2010

A Misted Mirror

Proverse Prize Joint-Winner 2010

by **Gillian Jones**

Proverse Hong Kong

A Misted Mirror
by Gillian Jones, 22 November 2011.
1st published in Hong Kong by Proverse Hong Kong, 22 November 2011.
Copyright © Proverse Hong Kong, 22 November 2011.
ISBN 978-988-19932-3-6

Distribution (Hong Kong and worldwide): The Chinese University Press of Hong Kong, The Chinese University of Hong Kong, Shatin, New Territories, Hong Kong, SAR.
E-mail: cup@cuhk.edu.hk Web site: www.chineseupress.com
Tel: [INT+852] 2609-6508; Fax: [INT+852] 2603-7355
Distribution (United Kingdom): Enquiries and orders to Christine Penney, 28 West Street, Stratford-upon-Avon, Warwickshire CV37 6DN, England.
Email: <chrisp@proversepublishing.com>
Additional distribution: Proverse Hong Kong, P. O. Box 259, Tung Chung Post Office, Tung Chung, Lantau Island, NT, Hong Kong, SAR, China.
E-mail: proverse@netvigator.com Web site: www.proversepublishing.com

The right of Gillian Jones to be identified as the author of this work has been asserted by her in accordance with the Copyright, Designs and Patents Act 1988. The right of Keith Jones to be identified as the author of the poems quoted at the beginning of each chapter is also asserted.

Copyright of the poems by Keith Jones quoted at the beginning of each chapter is owned by Gillian Jones. Please address any enquiries to her. Some of these poems have been published previously. Please see "Permissions".

Printed in Hong Kong by Artist Hong Kong Company, Unit D3, G/F, Phase 3, Kwun Tong Industrial Centre, 448-458, Kwun Tong Road, Kowloon, Hong Kong.
Page design by Proverse Hong Kong. Cover design, Pentacor Book Design.

Proverse Hong Kong

British Library Cataloguing in Publication Data

Jones, Gillian.
  A misted mirror.
  1. Parkinson's disease--Patients--Care--Fiction.
  2. Dementia--Patients--Care--Fiction. 3. Parkinson's
  disease--Patients--Family relationships--Fiction.
  4. Dementia--Patients--Family relationships--Fiction.
  5. Poets--Fiction. 6. Authors' spouses--Fiction.
  I. Title
  823.9'2-dc22

ISBN-13: 9789881993236

Permissions

With one exception the poems in *A Misted Mirror* are by Keith Jones, late husband of the author. The copyright of all Keith Jones's poems now belongs to Gillian Jones.

Of those of Keith Jones's poems that appear in *A Misted Mirror*, the following are previously unpublished: 'The Dreamer', 'Death', 'The Emperor', 'Raki'.

The following poems appeared previously in *Merrimans and other poems*, by Keith Jones, London, Agenda Editions, Poets and Painters Press, London, 2001, Limited edition of 250 copies: 'Koi' (*Merrimans,* p. 15), 'Ed' (*Merrimans,* p. 38), 'Presence' (*Merrimans,* pp. 66-67), 'Holly Bush Lane' (*Merrimans,* p. 65), 'The Tower' (*Merrimans,* p. 50), 'Only Yours' (*Merrimans,* p. 26), 'Alisoun' (*Merrimans,* pp. 42-43), 'Gates' (*Merrimans,* p. 16), 'The Coming of Rhiannon' (*Merrimans,* pp. 59-60).

The following poems were first published in *The Fool Faces 72*, published by Tetralith (in association with the Consortium of London Presses), 1975: 'The Lovers' (*The Fool Faces 72*, p. 6), 'Om' (*The Fool Faces 72*, p. 18), 'Towards the Feast' (*The Fool Faces 72*, p. 12). 'Om' later appeared also in *Merrimans,* p. 52. The version of 'Towards the Feast' included here is slightly different from that published in *The Fool Faces 72*.

'Oshogbo' was first published in *The London Magazine,* New Series April/May 1998, Vol. 38, Nos. 1 and 2 (page 31), and subsequently in *Merrimans and other poems* (p. 42).

First published in *Agenda,* Vol. 44, Nos 2-3, Spring 2009, were: 'Diyarbakr' (p. 78), and 'Prayers' (p. 77).

As quoted here, the texts are unaltered, except for one or two proof-reading points.

The extract quoted in Chapter 12 is from George Barker, 'Elegiac Sonnet for Tambi', published in *Tambimuttu – A Bridge Between Two Worlds* (p.107), edited and with a Preface by Jane Williams, Introduction by Robin Waterfield, Consultant Editor Kathleen Raine, London, Peter Owen, 1989. Included by kind permission of the Publishers.

This book is dedicated to the Admiral Nurses
a source of strength to carers.

CHAPTER TITLES AND CONTENTS

PROLOGUE

Koi
I was born here peering into Wales,
a crunch of marbles loaves beneath my feet;
to my left, the start of that prodigious
Saxon earthwork, Offa's dyke;
to my right, the Snowdon horizon
a crush of moon eggs and the glittering spire.

And soon the Norman church with its devil's door
opening onto the font, and the poor shack of a house
sharing the yew with the church,
the sweet red berries and toxic evergreen needles
on display, while underneath, the yew roots
threaded their necklace of skulls.

There's a thought for the girl at the sink
washing by the sputtering candle;
imagine, thought Koi, life is this
misted mirror and love the towelling
of the glass and breasts that jutter
like a wet nurse's ready to slake even the devil.

And out He dances, the devil,
walnut brown skin, eyes like sliced conkers.
Success for devils is sipping the sleeping breath;
girls then wake, candle guttering, their beauty gone.
They open their virgin palms. Not one journey can be read.
Follow mine, offers Koi, and with her finger

she copies his lifeline: – if not love then adventure.

Love or adventure: I could not tell you, even with hindsight, which
of those two I had wanted more. Or if the two were mutually
exclusive, although that was what the writer of the poem seemed to
suggest. Or maybe what I was looking for was something else
entirely. It was going to take time to find out what life's "misted

mirror" had been all about. I wanted urgently to understand where we were and how we had got here, to tell the wider world about that journey and to end the isolation of the place we had arrived at. The first thing was to decide where the narrative began.

That was easy as it started itself, quite naturally I think, one evening at the end of a day of caring when I sat down to write. More difficult was the question of who the narrator was, that person remembering the events and, for much of the time, living in the past. This was a double challenge, not just because of the unreliable nature of our memories but also the problem pure and simple of how to tell the story. The order in which you deploy your facts, the strands you select, the weight and prominence you give to each, all have to be weighed and considered. You write it one way but you could write it a hundred different ways, each with its shade of meaning, inviting subtly differing interpretations and judgements. Why did your character act in this way and not that way? Why were these thoughts going on in that head at that time? And how, in any case, could you know what was going on inside those heads? The narration becomes hedged around with caveats and qualifying clauses – on the one hand this and on the other hand maybe that. Add the thought that over the years the person telling the tale herself evolves and changes and then remind yourself that memory is unreliable and creates a narrative which changes the remembering, and the remembering is different each time because the act of recollection imposes a new layer of significance. Moreover, that fearful loss when memory itself becomes eroded with all the consequences to an individual's personality is another factor that has to be explored.

Memory deceives. What we think of as a true recollection turns traitor, and facts when checked up on, are shown to have been quite otherwise than what we would have sworn was the case. Our memories come in different shapes and sizes, in layers and hierarchies jostling for attention on competing levels. On one level are the events and sequences that we are quite certain about, on another the echoes of sensations and emotions recalled from far back and linked, Proustian-style, to sounds and scents, voices and places but with added layers of hindsight which alter them, for better or for worse Some are memories we care for, cherish and polish, adding an extra gloss as we do so, "precious moments", laughter, excitement, family moments captured in a photograph, with a particular sound track that goes with them. And yes, not to be forgotten or swept under the carpet, there are those awkward memories, the ones which you would prefer to gloss over but at times feel impelled to take out and with great caution examine and inspect.

With a deep distrust of memory and awareness of the pitfalls awaiting the first-person narrator, I personally am deterred from the attempt to tell this story and I have decided instead to hand the task over to "Sarah". "David" becomes the subject of the story and Sarah, the wife, is the one to tell it. Maybe we can take the facts on trust from Sarah as she recalls them, with a minimum of hesitation or self-interrogation. If the reader wants to question anyone about anything at all, let him or her question Sarah, as she begins the story.

HOMECOMING

July 2004

"Peter was looking well!"

David settled himself in the front passenger seat, fastening his seatbelt with a habitual movement. This was how it had always been when I picked him up from the airport; the two of us, David and Sarah, in the front with the children crowding happily in the back to welcome their father home.

I smiled, remembering that scene at the airport: the children searching for their father among the surge of passengers coming through the gates.

"Daddy! Daddy! Here he comes!" as they spotted him pushing his luggage trolley through the barrier in the Arrivals Hall. First he would carry the children to the car – one on the trolley and one on his shoulders. Then, on the drive home, he would report on mutual friends seen on the trip, comment on the children, our two boys, Joe and Nigel and their excited greetings. And so it was today.

"Peter was looking well!"

I kept silent, wondering which of the several Peters, among our friends and acquaintances, was in his mind as he continued.   "I thought Joe was quite delightful just now!"

I glanced across, puzzled, for Joe wasn't with us; today it was different and Joe, of course, was working in London.

All the same I smiled at him reassuringly. For today he hadn't been on a trip anywhere, had seen none of the Peters during the past week, today I was picking him up from the nursing home, to spend the weekend back at the house and no Joe or Nigel had greeted him just now, jumping up and down, calling "Daddy, Daddy", with impatience.

Today it was all in his head. Joe and Nigel were in their twenties, young men getting on with their lives in different ways and, in between that, sparing a thought, I hoped, to wonder about how their mother was coping.

The nursing home had been a desperate resort when I realized that I could no longer cope, at least not in a dignified way, with what I was beginning to call in my mind "the D-word": D for dementia. And, "in a dignified way" meant keeping calm and serene, when every impulse drove me to the opposite extreme, to behaviour which I saw with alarm was bordering on the abusive.

Perhaps abusive was too strong; it hadn't got to the stage of violence but was certainly, verbally, unkind. The times, for example when his apparent immobility appeared to be more wilful bloody-mindedness and a determination not to be helpful than the effects of his disease, those times when he stood stock-still, like a statue and transfixed, when only a moment ago hadn't he been hopping around the kitchen? Or in the bedroom, trying to get him dressed in the morning and he suddenly refused to move. Those were the moments when my temper snapped and, "Oh for Christ's sake David, why can't you bloody well put your own socks on!" escaped me as a moment of blessed relief. Or when the kitchen surfaces were smeared with ice-cream and honey, with cocoa-powder, marmalade and banana, where he had made himself a dessert in the short space of time I had given myself to nip outside to walk the dog and cool my temper. As I came back in to find the scene, the kitchen a sticky mess and the full tub of ice cream a sloshy, yellow liquid I failed to restrain my exasperation.

"I shan't be shopping for ice-cream again till Friday, so you'll just have to go without for the rest of the week!" I snapped at his retreating back and then, going through to the sitting room found him on the floor, where he had over-balanced, thankfully not with the dessert in his hand, this time at any rate, but his drink splashed on the carpet.

"Come on, up you get!" I held out a hand to pull him up, not roughly, but not kindly either, except that he was too big and too heavy for me to raise him up and the last time I had let him use me as a lever he had crushed the joint in my forefinger, the unmentionable arthritic joint which lurked quiescent but, once knocked or crushed caused pain and irritation for the next three weeks and which, on top of the ice-cream and marmalade-smeared kitchen and the constant need to remind him of which day of the week it was and that we were not due to fly to Abu Dhabi or Singapore and did not need passports or tickets or a suitcase, and the constant searches to find his walking stick – a necessity which got left everywhere and his wallet, which was his ultimate, climactic, and totally panic-inducing obsession: on top of all that it was the inflamed and aching finger joint which prevented me from putting him out of my mind even when out of the house and out of sight.

The poems fuelled my anger too; take this one for instance:
"in your own spaces
let the winds fetch
clean clouds
that you may stay gentle."

"*Gentle!*" Yes, indeed, some time ago. These days bad-tempered, resentful, burdened with self-pity described me better, a person I hardly recognized, and whom I most thoroughly disliked.

And so it had come to pass that, with the help and advice of the District Nurse and a Care Manager, I had taken the staggering move of convincing David that he would be alright in a nursing home – at least for a trial period, and he could come home for weekends – well, most weekends perhaps. I had stuffed the remnants of my guilt far down, subjecting them to the rationality of the nurse: "We don't want the two of you going under, do we? One is bad enough!"

I had almost kept up that façade as I transported him there, unloaded his television, his clothes, books, various small items of comfort, photographs of myself and boys and had left him there in a blur of tears that witnessed not so much to my grief at leaving him as my grief for the whole sad tragedy of how our lives, at the outset so exciting, had come to this sorry pass.

At the home the nurses were not particularly kind; not unkind but just overburdened with rules and regulations – OK, I thought, that was putting it charitably, some of them were downright bitchy. The Dutch nurse was the most sympathetic, especially towards me, repeating over and over, "What a tragedy for David, so intelligent! It always happens to the intelligent ones! And good-looking too!" And, "What a hard, hard life for the wives," she had continued, and on, and on, and on, making me feel even more sorry for myself. Another nurse, burly with a joshing sense of humour and a figure like a bricklayer, was sympathetic in a different way:

"Do you know, when you came in here first, you looked as if you were ready either to cut his throat or your own!"

"Was I as bad as that? I suppose I must have been."

Then there was the nurse who assumed she knew far better than I did about every aspect of David and his treatment: the medication, the routine, the underlying symptoms, the reasons for irrationality and it was difficult to resist snapping back at her, "Yes, I know that actually, I've been looking after him for the last ten years!" And once, once only, I had failed to resist the temptation to snap at her and relations with that particular nurse had deteriorated. Finally there was the manager, the one you had to defer to because she had made the decision to accept David into the home and was going to keep a close eye on how he settled in. She was clearly uneasy.

"He's walking around the corridors all day, in and out and going into people's rooms," she told me. "It's the short-term memory trying to function" she explained with an experienced nod. "He'll be alright as soon as he's got it sorted in his mind where he is and who everyone else is." I feared that the restlessness was something different, but I kept silent on the matter, hoping that he would indeed settle.

And it did seem for a while as if that might be the case. After a month or so, when I brought him back to the nursing home after a weekend at home, he had settled into his armchair and given me a truly angelic smile. "Welcome to my home! This is my home now!"

And that too, infuriatingly, had brought tears of pity again to my eyes.

Now in the car he was happy to be heading for home: just like in the old times when, at the end of a long week away from home, when I picked him up from the airport he would settle back in the car, contented.

"Peter was looking well! And Jo was charming just now."

I smiled at him. Moving the engine into gear, I set off for home.

At home – our home – David sat in the recliner chair in his accustomed corner of the sitting room, happy to be back there with a cup of tea at his elbow.

"Tablets first!" I gave him two, one yellow, one white and a drink of water then handed him a plate with chocolate cake and a napkin.

"Now. Your poems! Shall I read this one?"
"Fine. Yes please!" He smiled contentedly.

EXPLORING NORTHERN NIGERIA

Ed
You lived just up the red track, our properties abutting.
We shared the monitor lizards, the small black violent
snakes, nightwatchman with bow, arrow, bicycle,
gardeners with scimitar blades and quick reaction times.
We also shared *in loco parentis* – your peace corps,
my volunteers. And then there were our wives.

They were much the same in build. But colour – ah!
Mine was blonde now, natural sunbleached straw;
before, scandinavian white silk. Yours was hair
brushed by ravens; skin, a Persian peach. Tongues were
instructive too. Yours had, in her small mouth, this pink
flicker as though the tip, worried by the chasm

between our mouths, would bring the word nearer.
She wouldn't, of course. Mine though put tongues
in other people's mouths ahead of speech. Her intelligence was,
you may say, kinaesthetic. Hers was not a talking face.
She played silent theatre. With make-up that faked
that post-coital cheekflush, but kept the eyes

a daughter green. Yours – let's call her Liz – was,
I guess, a trifle more perfunctory. She had
that jackie kennedy smile to flash, and when she did
hyperbole took her. Lucky hyperbole. And you,
Ed. Mine's but a small box of smiles – the wistful silence,
patience on a monument, the bony shouldered one.

Both their walks unstitch the knees. Those rotational
collisions, mock dislocations of the hip. As below, so above.
But below's ahead. The expanding universe has yet to meet
its twin. And when it does, and the duopoly stands up
and learns to walk, what sights, what sonnets,
What godlets in what new dimensions agape?

OK Ed. My turn behind the wheel.

"Ed"... David had written that poem ten years ago, when the disease was beginning to take hold. What I called his "executive powers" were getting slower; he was finding it difficult to handle meetings and to work under pressure and meet deadlines – features of his work which he had relished up to then. For years the Organisation which he worked for in cultural relations had been like family to him but now early retirement came as a relief. It brought him release from the pain of the anxiety that he was unable to perform in his old assured way. And in compensation, for a few years his brain made up for the loss of those abilities with a renewed flowering of creative powers.

I read the poem through with closer attention than before and a different kind of attention, admitting to myself that I hadn't done so up till now, partly I supposed, because of the intimations of a life – in particular intimations of a sex-life – that I felt I was very definitely being asked not to enquire about. It was hard to imagine that life in the nineteen-seventies when David was posted to Northern Nigeria with his beautiful but somewhat reluctant first wife. I did wonder if perhaps she hadn't seen much future to her career as a dancer in that part of the world and whether that had been the cause of resentment. And now David was unable to tell me much at all.

"Was the house a bungalow?" I asked, trying to get him started.

That much he agreed. Yes, a bungalow.

"And who was Ed?"

But he had trouble even with speech now. Words would not come; they stuck on his tongue and the vocal chords failed to respond to the will of the brain.

"Ed was the American c-c-c-consul" came the stuttered reply. I had known that before, hadn't I? Of course, Ed, the American consul!

As nothing more was forthcoming I brought him a bowl of ice-cream (I couldn't keep up with the consumption of ice-cream these days) and poured sweet maple syrup on it, then turned my thoughts to the poem and what I knew of its circumstances.

So, a bungalow, Africa, 1970....
The bungalow was set back from a wide and dusty street, David had said, situated just off Ahmadu Bello Avenue, a road of red

dust, pot-holed pavements, compacted red earth and gravel, and here and there the remnants of a former paved surface. The road was lined with similar residences, each with its garden, some tended, green, well-watered and cared for, others quietly neglected. The properties were inhabited mostly by middle class local and expatriate businessmen and their families. This one was a slab-fronted bungalow and its garden was of the quietly neglected type. Out front there were trees, also dusty, leaning in grotesque shapes, providing shade for the garden boy. Canna lilies, also dust-covered, offered a jaunty, gaudy welcome. And there was the garden boy – in my imagination I saw him – snoozing in the shade of the tree, awake enough to whisk away the flies, ignoring the monitor lizards, which inhabited the wall that divided the garden from next door's, abutting theirs, up the red track. His hand lay lightly on the machete at his side and would deal swiftly, more swiftly than the eye could follow, with any small, black, violent snake that came seeking coolness inside the house.

Inside the house – *what*? I wondered as I read. *Inside it must surely be cooler*. There isn't any air conditioning – or if there is it's not switched on – but a ceiling fan swishes rhythmically, rustling the light-weight curtains and creating its own quiet, unhurried, nothing's-going-to-happen-for-a-long-time-yet, peace and calm. A houseboy flicks a duster over some low tables, straightens three soft, grey, leather sofas, emptying the overflowing ashtrays, and collects up tumblers with the dregs of last night's drinks. Books are returned to bookshelves. Gin and whisky bottles are tidied up – the duty-free brand from the Embassy stores, with the tops off –and half-used small bottles of soda and ginger ale – (*bottles, not cans*, I think to myself; *you didn't get ginger ale or soda in cans in the seventies, did you*?)

LPs are slipped into their record sleeves. (*Can the boy read English? Does he know which record goes in which sleeve*?)

The houseboy works quietly, treats each item circumspectly and, although the house is quiet there must be someone else around for him to treat the items with such respect. Working away, he mops up spills, returns the tops to bottles, clears the empties onto a tray, takes them out to … (*the kitchen, the pantry? Perhaps we'll get to see that later*) ….to wash and put away.

Certainly the house isn't empty. The wife is there! So what was she doing? Sleeping late? She's been doing her nail varnish; toes as well as fingers and here she comes, negligee reaching right the way down – to her mid thighs... (*Well it's the seventies isn't it? The mini-skirt era: and anyway, the humidity must be unbearable!*) ....and blowing on her finger nails. She has showered and shampooed. The sun-bleached straw hair is nearly dry and ruffles as she passes under the ceiling fan. The make-up is perfect: that cheek-bone high flush contrasting with the egg-shell matt finish below, dark eye-liner and generous lashes enhancing the innocence of green eyes. The houseboy worships her. She drops him a word, to make his morning and to get him out of her way. "Thanks Peter, that's OK. I'll have a coffee."

"Yes madam, thank you madam. Coffee coming." And he hurries out to spoon the Nescafé into the cup and open a tin of condensed milk.

Hmm, yes. That's how it was.

And now, nearly 12.30 by the clock on the drinks cabinet. Dave will be back for lunch and siesta soon. The humidity is rising and equalled by the rising din of the cicadas outside before they switch off for the torpor of the afternoon. *Ah Nigeria in the nineteen seventies! The decade of development, when aid was flowing in and aid-workers were carefree and took long lunch-hours.*

Now, all at once the screech of brakes in the road outside as, in joyous mood Dave skids to a halt in front of "the Bung", leaps out and abandons the car, chucking the keys to the garden boy, whose treat it is to drive the green Cortina, his pride and joy, round to the back and reverently wash the red dust from its paintwork and wheels.

Tall, curly-haired, bespectacled, swinging his briefcase he strides up the path, past the cannas – always his favourite – ducking under the twisted branches of the acacia to burst in the door upon her with a "Ta-ra! – back again! How's my Sugar?"

She shakes her viscous red nails at him indicating to keep off her whilst they dry, but he is peeling off his jacket, unzipping his flies and bouncing her onto the soft, grey leather sofa, for all the world as if he hasn't had her for a fortnight, let alone three times before work that morning.

"For Christ's sake" she mutters, succumbed but not responding, and the kitchen boy, catching her reproving eye retreats to the kitchen, but makes sure to leave the door lightly ajar. Sure, garden boy gets to drive the car but kitchen boy has stories of another kind to hold an audience spellbound.

The soft sofa responds with sighs of expelled air from its well-upholstered cushions. They are shiny and slippery, becoming shinier and slipperier with each groan and sigh and giggle and exclamation until couple and cushions lie together in flagrant disarray on the shaggy rug on the glacial hardness of the polished stone-tiled floor. After an eloquent and satisfied pause in the proceedings, Dave pulls himself up and off her, cracking his head on the low coffee table.

"Ouch! – Damn!" and she begins delicately to put herself together, inspecting each part like a cat licking its fur.

"Now look what you've done! My nails are ruined. It's on your shirt too!" She tries to pull his shirt tails round to show him where the bright red nail varnish had stained.

"Careless Sugar!" he reproves her,

"Careless – Me! Who's talking? And look at the sofa!"

"Ah." That seems to reach him; the soft leather sofa was his own choosing; the fulfillment of a very private dream of luxury; as indeed is the mid-day fucking of his Sugar-Plum fairy on the soft grey surface, another private fulfillment. But red nail-varnish on soft grey leather? No, definitely not.

"Nail-varnish remover; where is it?"

"Finished" she mutters crossly, rearranging her wispy negligee that he has so avidly disrobed her of and searching around for the panties, which he has twirled around and flicked over the sofa back.

"Peter!" he calls "Fetch nail-varnish remover – right now!" The kitchen boy stares, bemused.

"Varnish-remover – for this! Look! For cleaning!" There follows a pantomime as he leads the boy to the sofa, indicating the red marks, sniffing them, holding the boy's face to sniff, then grabbing her hand to show him the varnish and indicate the nature of the stains to be cleaned.

"Varnish-remover! Go – buy – clean sofa – OK?"

Light dawns for Peter who smiles and nods.

"Go, buy, clean!"

"Good!"

"Need money!"

"Ah," and Dave pats his sides looking for change but, finding only shirt looks around for trousers which lie on the floor, along with underpants too. Grabbing the trousers he throws them for Peter to catch.

"Money here. Go; buy; clean sofa. OK?"

Peter grins, gathering up the trousers. Making for the door he bends to retrieve a lacy ball which lies in his path and, unraveling the panties, he turns to present them but unsure whether it should be to him or to her, the offering, spreads them reverently, delicately, avoiding the red stains of the nail-varnish, on the arm of the grey leather sofa, regards them as an artist might his craft work then leaves the room, closing the door properly this time behind him; he has stories enough.

"Right!" Dave is in shirt tails and socks and happy that the grey leather will in due course be restored. Good too that the boy is out of the house, not that it bothers him, only for her sake.... She is dishevelled, standing there still: pantyless – just how he likes her!

"OK Sugar – let's go!

Dave and Ed were sitting at the bar with tankards of ale, heads together. It was clearly a good topic of conversation for at intervals Dave leant back on his bar stool with a guffaw and slapping of thighs and Ed rocked back and forth gesturing to emphasise a point. Two more glasses, set out on the bar, showed that they were not planning to drink alone. The two women appeared, fastening their handbags and patting their hair, they stood in the archway to the bar, pausing together to watch their men deep in conversation. Ed glanced up.

"Hi sweetheart!" he called to the dark one, "Over here!"

The girls held their pose in the archway for a calculated few seconds, enough to allow the other occupants of the room to turn their heads and take in the vision, then advanced together as if on a catwalk, pelvises rolling, a hand on the hip, heads posed symmetrically, leaning out.

Sugar had exchanged her flimsy negligee for a shocking pink mini-skirt, flattering skinny top and high sling-back sandals. She did justice to all of them. Liz favoured the Jackie Kennedy look with contour-clinging shift dress ending well short of the knees by about eight inches, Dave reckoned appraisingly although it was hard to calculate, even giving it his best attention (which he invariably did), because her legs just went on and on.

The girls were well-matched, if a contrasting pair can be called a match: Liz's dark, raven-haired beauty, wide-brown eyes and flashing smile contrasting with Sugar's beach-blonde colouring and more sultry look. Both had the dancer's grace with the model's eye for the effect they were creating.

And quite some effect it was too; the other occupants of the bar were visibly impressed. What were these exotic birds doing in this place? Most wives were at the Golf Club or recovering from morning coffee parties but these two didn't fit the normal description for wives: were they the real thing? As if sensing the question in the air around the bar Ed put an arm protectively and proprietarily around Liz's waist. Dave was unaware of the ambiguity and slapped Sugar's bottom which made her scowl which in turn dented his bonhomie and turned the corners of his mouth down, momentarily, with a puzzled look.

Why was she like this to him? Why not all flashing smile like her friend? Who he must admit was rather gorgeous and to whom he addressed himself now. "So, are you coming on the trip Liz?"

"Which trip would that be Dave?"

"You know which trip Liz," Ed chipped in, "the Peace Corps. Checking out the guys down there are OK."

"Girls as well as guys, Ed. I've got three girl VSOs to visit."

"Guys embraces girls – in US-speak, didn't you know that?"

"Too true Ed! Not just in USA-speak but in every other way," returned Dave. "Isn't that right Liz?" He turned to her.

"I guess you could say that girls embrace guys too," she returned. Her accent fascinated Dave. Just to hear those transatlantic vowels rolling off that flickering pink tongue as the wide smile flashed and the warm eyes invited made him reach for his ale to cool and calm the senses, and he waited for more.

"Depends who the guy is though," and she crossed her arms and leant towards him on the bar.

Dave looked on himself as the wordsmith but for a moment his vocabulary failed him as her perfume took over and his senses stopped the power of word in their tracks. Incredible!! Out of this world! Lucky old Ed!

"Yes, well, are you coming on the trip? The two of you could both come." He turned to find Sugar not just sultry now but sulky too.

"Six hours at least in the back of the car on those dreadful roads? No thanks; I've done it once and that's enough. Not for me, I'll stay here."

"But what will you do for four days on your own?"

"You're coming, aren't you sweetheart?" Ed put to Liz,

"I guess I'll just stay. Sugar and I can keep each other company. We'll have to trust the two of you on your own."

So two days later saw Dave and Ed in Ed's battered Toyota jeep setting off before dawn, hoping to get the worst of the drive over before it got too unbearably hot. He left a sleepy Sugar under the mosquito netting in the bedroom where the fan swished evenly overhead. He had snuggled up to her. "Just a few cuddles before I go Sugar: come on." But she was not to be coaxed. Feeling him stiffening and hardening against her back she pulled away.

"You'd better get going, Ed will be waiting"

"Be a good Sugar then, till I get back." She curled up in a ball, waiting till she heard the door slam and the sound of Ed's jeep pulling away, before she relaxed. Really, he was too demanding and never knew when to leave well alone. Anyway, she had lots to do while he was away. And a few more hours' sleep would be good.

Out on the road the sky was lightening, dawn would soon break. They were well away from the town and met few vehicles on the road. Down below the darkness was still absolute except where a few lights showed that villages were waking and fires were being lit. Ed had the radio on and Dave attempted to retune to a different station. It was African music, quite good fun but pity Ed's jeep didn't have a tape-player. Now the Cortina would have been better in that respect and they could have listened to some real music – Stones or Beatles. As the sun came up Dave decided it was time for a break and a change.

"Time to stop for a bite Ed and then – *my turn behind the wheel*!"

Some involuntary movement had jerked David's arm and the hand holding the mug of tea sending the warm liquid splashing over his jacket and the arm of the chair. I put the book of poems down and went to the kitchen for a cloth to mop up.

"No harm done. Another poem?"

He nodded.

"This will be the last one," I warned him, "I've got things to do."

EMBROIDERING ON FLOWERS

Oshogbo (1970)
Nigerian English colloquium over
and in this palmwine drinkers' bar
just thirty yards of sweat from the hotel,

the wine sliding slowly down you as you look
out from all the flowers in your frock
tongue tending your rolled back lips.

I guess you are a safe seventeen, imagine you
sticky as palm-wine. Let's go, and we did,
and your lips pulled.

First hotel trip! You were so taken with the gleam
of tiles and porcelain and all of you in this wallmirror –
it wasn't me that prompted the undress!

And so to bath, with shaving soap for foam.

Football would provide the grand finale of the two-day get-
together in Oshogbo, the Peace Corps versus the VSOs. But first
there was serious stuff to get through.

Dave and Ed had come loaded with supplies. They included
poster paints, magic markers, a crate of pots of schoolroom glue,
piles of old magazines. In addition they had brought crates of
tinned sausages, baked beans and sardines; the latter were
especially appreciated – something about their saltiness, and you
could do a lot with mashed sardines. And crates of beer of course;
Heineken providing a welcome change from the local brew. Since
it was the first week of school holidays the colloquium had been
arranged at the Oshogbo Secondary Girls High. The volunteers,
young idealists taking a year out from their studies or before
starting their careers, had been bussed in from the schools where
they were teaching in outlying villages and townships. After their
first few months they were more than ready for a break. The
British wore the VSO badge of Voluntary Service Overseas and

the Americans that of the American Peace Corps. They arrived in twos and threes, fired by the thought of getting together again and meeting new faces and more than ready for some rest and relaxation after their strenuous first term's work.

Oshogbo, promoted as Arts capital of Central Nigeria, held its attractions. They included a sculpture park, a museum, a theatre and enough clubs and bars to keep everyone happy. The volunteers were staying at the two-star Majestic Hotel. Dave and Ed were at the 4-star Oasis and the teachers would be invited there for drinks in the evening.

First on the programme, Dave's Workshop, on "Using Magazine Pictures" with a film of two ladies in action with the mag-pics which never failed to charm and inspire, followed by a happy hour when Brits and Americans cut and pasted and did clever Blue Peter things with cardboard. Then Dave was let loose with his lecture: "Theories of Language Acquisition: some implications for teaching English in Nigerian Bush Schools". Ed was no linguist and brought them down to earth with a workshop on story-telling. He started with a story about a cab-driver and a long-distance trucker. Inevitably trans-Atlantic word-war broke out and accusations [correct word?] of trucker versus lorry-driver, boot and trunk, bonnet and hood, fanned the flames. The teachers went away in groups to work on their own story-telling sessions and to polish them up ready for performance in the Arts Theatre. This was Cultural Diplomacy in enthusiastic action.

The second day was spent in rehearsal, with Dave doing most of the work while Ed looked on in some surprise at the way things came together. As voice-coach, producer and director, Dave's approach consisted of turning the workshop into a cauldron of ideas and activity. Into this pot he would throw eccentric ideas for the teams who picked them up with enthusiasm, quite quickly turning them into acts for the evening's show. Dave was everywhere, encouraging, demonstrating, putting his feet up with one of the teams and sitting back while they all ran around and did impossible things with the fire that he had lit.

In the evening the Arts Theatre was full and buzzing, for Ed had made sure that the event was publicized. There were local businessmen wearing robes and carrying ceremonial fly-whisks with wives in extravagant dresses with puffed sleeves and head-dresses of stiffly-ironed and skillfully wound taffeta, ex-pat heads of businesses, Reckitts, Pepsi and Shell, all the local businesses, bringing along those younger children not yet away at boarding schools. And the Press was there, Ed had made sure of that, supplying a press release for those pushed for time.

Five short stories were presented in dramatized form for maximum audience involvement, which was enthusiastically contributed by most of the audience, who, talking and laughing, streamed out of the theatre at the end of the evening's pleasant entertainment.

Half an hour of buying the performers drinks in the Oasis Hotel bar left Ed and Dave feeling they were using up their entertainment allowance too quickly. A move towards bed was suggested; some complied, others drifted away to carry out more research into Oshogbo nightlife. Dave found himself with the latter group. Kerry and Jane were two VSOs stationed in a school only ten miles from the town. He had noticed them together as a pair, Kerry round and small with red curly hair and freckles, her chubby bottom wiggling a lot in the barely decent mini-skirt. Jane wore her light brown hair in a pony tail, lots of jangly bracelets and this evening, for the night-club, she was wearing an all-in-one sort of romper suit of the kind which, Dave had noticed in Sugar's magazines recently, were provocatively labeled hot pants. Dave was very susceptible to provocatively-named items of clothing, believing in the suggestive power of words to reinforce the seductive power of the flesh which they failed to conceal. The curious thing about the hot pants suit was how, should the occasion ever arise, would one go about removing it?

But the thing about VSOs, as Ed reminded Dave, was that one was there to look after them. Ed, joining them at the bar was trailed by his own set of Peace Corps, three men, six girls all looking fresh out of school – but a safe seventeen all the same.

Noting the pensive reverie of Dave contemplating hot pants Ed murmured in his ear.

"Hey man, *in loco parentis*, remember? Better forget about it! You're on duty right now!"

"Ah; you are too right! And a duty shared is a duty halved – right?"

"Too right: share and share alike, but wait till the Colloquium is over"

"Hmm; lunch time tomorrow then. No hurry about the return journey?"

By lunch-time the next day the final plenary session had been held, the honours presented, congratulations shared and thanks gracefully delivered to sponsors. Dave found himself surrounded by a group of faces eager to carry him along with them to the palm drinkers' bar they had discovered the night before. The midday heat was intense and the five minutes' walk was enough to make the dive into the bar a welcome relief. Anglo-American relationships were now at an all time high and the young Peace Corps couple monopolized Dave, quizzing him about where they could stay in London when their year was over and they were on their way back home. Glancing across, Dave saw Ed similarly surrounded by the VSOs, loving his California accent and engaging him with their questions about his home state.

"Well, San Francisco, that's a place you ought to get to see while you can; while you still have flowers in your hair." Jane, Dave noticed was gazing at Ed in awe. Talking of flowers, she had swapped the hot pants for a frilled frock of brilliant flowers with a collar that stood up at the back and cradled her face like some Renaissance Venus looking out from her frame. Pre-empting any intention Ed might have, Dave moved across to her.

"How's the palm-wine going down?"

He had surprised her; she jumped and choked and in a startled riot of giggles spluttered palm-wine down the front of her frock.

"Now look what you've done!" she giggled and held back her head to lick her lips and catch the drops from her cheek with her tongue. Dave had manoeuvred them aside and took advantage of the head held back to show solicitous concern for the rest of the wine as it ran down her front. Head bent forward, tongue reached the cleavage, drops of wine were skilfully retrieved and scents and promise of more registered, in two as if in one. Her head came forward, startled. Dave was at her elbow.

"This way I think." He motioned towards the door. Ed raised his eyebrows, registering the departure. The wine-drinking continued as the sound levels rose inside the bar.

Outside, the street was even hotter and sweat mingled with the remnants of wine. The Oasis Hotel was not fifty yards from the palm-wine bar and its cool air-conditioned interior came as a shock. Kerry shivered – from cold? And in the lift the usual awkward moment passed when Dave turned her to face the mirrors while he leant from behind to finish the job of removing remnants of wine from her cleavage. She shrieked with delight at the transition. From lift to bedroom was a carpeted muffled few steps which passed in another wave of giggles as a chambermaid beat a hasty retreat from arranging the bathroom. They would soon disarrange it!

She tried the bed; the mattress was springy: a VSO's dream.

"Wow, I'd forgotten what a real bed was like! And this is phenomenal!" she exclaimed. "Let me see the bathroom!"

Then from the bathroom.

"Oh my God! How about this for a joyride?"

He followed her in, loosening his shirt on the way, to find Kerry gazing at the mirror-paneled interior, the shiny bath-tub, the gleam of tiles and porcelain.

His arms around her shoulders, they contemplated their image. As Dave leant over to drink more wine she addressed him in the mirror.

"No more of that, but what about.... well, how about..." an enquiring look as she led his hands to the neat shirt-waister buttons and the flowered frock dropped its petals to the floor. She liked what she saw in the mirror, was pleased and unabashed at her pretty body; Dave liked it even more.

It seemed a good idea to fill the bath, and a moment later the spray was everywhere, and once the bath was filled and clothes discarded, another good idea was shaving foam. And so to bath, with foam, caressing bodies and laughter, subsiding satisfactorily.

Yes, I reflected, putting the poem aside, *that's probably how it was. I may have embroidered a bit, but, on the whole, that's probably a fairly accurate picture!*

WINTER SOLSTICE

Presence
It was one of those improbable zoological
moments when you sense
there are two of you, kangaroo pouched

inhabiting the same space, the same kirlian net,
both kitchen grazing in silence so delicate
not even the snap of an occasional dragon

nor rasping lick of frozen burdock abrades.
Chomping globes of garlic, the screech of mandrake.
(*Mandragora, orange poppyroot, the thunderflower*).

An eyelid flick and the kitchen's once more
devoid of kangaroo, and you – disconcerted,
skinned, raw, cloven-tongued, idolic –

hungrily search among such signs as
tall invisible mammals,
presences – angelic or other;

ba, my double, stumbles me across the broken house
and renders visible the *genius loci* – white freaked up hair
stooping between dimensions,

hook in hand collecting the redsnot
gobble berries of the yew; the fleshy red cups,
he tells, are sticky sweet and safe, but the seeds,

the seeds are toxic, heart slows,
gut collapses. Quarter of an hour,
that's all the time you can reckon.

In the first Zoo a dazed ostrich fed on yew berries
allows a plucking of its feathers. In the second Zoo
justice with sword and scale.

Zoos twitter with the recent dead.
Sideshows display; one legged rain dance,
the knotty testicles of orchids,

Monk's Hood – the old woman in her bed –
cherubic storms. Hot snow falling.
Signs becoming beings becoming signs.

December 2004

21st of December: the winter solstice. A time when strange things happen, when things can fall apart.

It had been exactly six months ago, I realized, that David had gone to the Nursing Home, June 21st. Midsummer is a time of energy and aspiration. Then in September it became apparent that it wasn't working and David had to come home, with all that meant in terms of caring.

Now in winter it was a time to keep strong nerves, even if, outside, the light was draining away, spiraling like the last dregs of water from a tub, leaving a black hole that threatened to drag me in too.

Keep your nerve, I thought, put lights in the windows, candles indoors, dispel rash words and actions, stay calm.

Last night I hadn't stayed calm at all. David had been at home again for three months now following the failed trial months in a nursing home and I felt utterly trapped. Sleepless, in the middle of the night, in my mind I had plotted escape and had got it all worked out. And here today the notes made in the middle of the night were on the table to prove it, prepared like a prompt card, ready to confront the specialist we would be seeing today who wanted to withdraw some of David's tablets, a move which I vehemently opposed. His visit was expected and I looked through my notes again.

"One – To change David's medication at this stage is unreasonable and unworkable.
"Two – My ability to cope is on a knife edge; if you want to withdraw the tablets it should be done under supervision and that means in hospital.

"Three – I've already tried it for a couple of days and without the tablets the Spooks return straight away.
"Four – I need a new prescription today. My alternative is to leave the house this afternoon when you do; I've got it worked out and will go to friends."

In the light of the morning this melodramatic threat sounded hollow and unreal but the frantic, scrappy notes bore witness to the stress of the night before.

"Spooks", when they occurred, were an acute problem; unwanted strangers which appeared to David, turning up in corners, sitting brazenly in an armchair, keeping him silent company. At these moments David took on a timorous demeanour, unsure of who they were or what they were doing, for how long and at whose invitation. Their first appearance was when the two boys were still in school. I came home one evening to find Joe puzzled and uneasy, while David had taken himself off to the sitting room.

"Dad said there had been people here: not sure exactly when… before we came back"

"Really? Who?" I asked.

"He said they were from the Czech Republic. Then he said Poland…I couldn't get it really… He asked me to get some beers from the fridge for them."

I frowned.

"Did he say who they were?"

Joe shook his head.

"Actually I didn't see anyone was here… unless they had left by then."

I was already going through to the sitting room.

"What's this about people from Poland, David?"

David had poured himself a drink; he was looking flushed and his hair was fluffed up as if he had been running his hands through it, but he spoke quite calmly in a matter-of-fact way.

"Yes, they were here."

"Who? Who was here?"

"From Central Europe…. You know, where I was…." He tailed off, looking at me expectantly, as if he expected me to join in, to engage.

"It was a café; we were just having some drinks!"

Well, David had made various trips to Poland and Central European countries in his last role with the Organisation before he retired and it was not outside the realms of possibility that one of his contacts from those days had in reality made a call. It seemed unlikely though.

That was my first encounter with the phenomenon which we were later to call "Spooks". I could sense the confusion in David's head because, although he appeared convinced of their reality, he refused later in the evening to be drawn on the subject at all. A few days later David had gone up to bed, early as was his habit these days, and when I went up at about 10.30 I found him sitting up in bed, his eyes round and staring, pulling himself towards the back of the bed away from whatever was threatening him, clearly terrified.

"Stop the thing!" he whispered in a cracked voice. The duvet was piled up in a big lump and he pushed vigorously at it with his feet. I rushed to catch it, looking for anything hidden within, which might be causing such distress, I could see nothing. I smoothed it out.

"What's happened with it?"

He shook his head and pointed. The duvet cover was a rather hectic pattern of browns and yellows and beiges – not the most beautiful; I think it had been a bargain which I had fallen for in a sale, with hindsight a disastrous buy. Anyway it had fallen on the floor by now and I picked it up and folded it. David's staring eyes blinked, several times and his breathing, which had been rapid and shallow, slowed down although his face was still flushed and his body language was tense and fearful. After a while he was able to explain to me that he had seen snakes and sea creatures, slimy monsters — he seemed to imply with his gestures — writhing up out of the duvet, twisting and twining: no wonder that he was terrified.

It became clear that such apparitions could create themselves out of innocent patterned material, wallpaper or carpets. While I felt I could understand and cope, I didn't want the boys to have to do the same whenever I was out. I wasn't sure how to explain it to them. Anyway, when I suggested that the medication might have something to do with these episodes they took it a lot more calmly than I had expected.

"What do you expect Mum, with all those tablets? They are *drugs* after all!"

I agreed and added, let it be a lesson to them!

The name – "Spooks" – was my own idea, my attempt to make light of the apparitions and to take the threat out of the experience. In earlier days David had enjoyed such verbal jokes and I hoped that by personifying them in this way I could remind David of their unreality. "*KEEPING THE SPOOKS AT BAY*" was what the tablets did.

The underlying cause of these appearances was harder to determine. According to the neurologist, in some cases it was in the nature of the illness, in other cases it was the medication for the illness that had the side effect of ushering in the apparitions. In David's case, after various trials it became clear that the medication gave rise to the spooks, so a cap was put on their use and more tablets were prescribed to dampen the unwanted effects of the first tablets. And to compensate for the tablets he could no longer take, David was given a new medication, delivered subcutaneously, under the skin of his stomach from a syringe powered by a small pump that fitted into his shirt pocket. Each morning the district nurse came to insert the needle.

Later, when I was shown how simple it was, I took that on as well and would set up the pump in the morning and take it down every evening, massaging the hard nodules which the medication created under the skin and the sore spot which it left behind.

That was five years ago. Now in midwinter, the new specialist was saying that the additional tablets, the "spook tablets", as I thought of them, might actually have other harmful side-effects and should be withdrawn. It was to be done gradually, over weeks, if necessary replacing them with other medication. The whole process, I reckoned, would take a month, but on day two the spooks returned, sinister guests in his bedroom at three in the morning.

The sound of David moving in his room in the middle of the night woke me. I went through and gently soothed him.

"Look, there's nothing there. I promise you!" By walking around, filling all the spaces of the room, sitting in the chair where he had "seen" the guest, I could demonstrate that there was indeed nothing or no-one there. The phantoms dispelled I got David back into bed and ready to sleep again. The next day I resumed giving him the tablets.

But now on the 21st of December – the winter solstice, I reflected, shortest and darkest day of the year – the tablets had run out and I had to ask for more.

"Please, I really need a fresh supply – today!" I told the doctor when he visited. "You know how fraught things get at Christmas."

He looked doubtful. "Couldn't you give it a bit longer? Just to see if he will adapt?"

But I knew I couldn't handle it.

"The family will be here" I explained. "If David is seeing a house full of strangers as well, and if I've been up half the night because of them, none of us will be on speaking terms by the end of the holiday."

There was no argument; the doctor wrote the prescription. He wasn't really there to make life more difficult for me, I reflected, although sometimes it seemed like it: in fact quite the opposite; and his support had made all the difference. It wasn't necessary to have got so worked up; all the same, a night's sleep had been needlessly lost.

"Do we know why it happened?"

The day before Christmas Eve David's friend Colin had come down to see his old friend. His visits were regular and always welcome. They provided good cheer and a valuable feeling of solidarity. After the meal and while David snoozed, Colin helped me in the kitchen.

"Do we know why what happened?" I asked.

"This! This... *disease*; if that's what you call it. It's the wrong name, to me. A disease is something you can see. Something like, well like the plague! That was a disease: boils and discoloured skin and scabs and things. But this; it's just a kind of crumbling away; an un-learning of everything he was good at."

"They call it a degenerative disease." I told him. "Everything degenerates! Nowadays I have to show him how to fasten a button or a shoe-lace. As for the radio or the television controller – don't even think of it!"

"How about the computer?" Colin asked. "He used it a lot before...."

"When his handwriting became illegible he used the computer for composing onto," I replied. "I watched that go downhill over the course of two to three years. It's been out of the question for a year or more." Colin smiled sadly. I was in full flow now, it was such a relief to be able to tell someone about the frustrations and the guilt of caring for David.

"During that time he wanted so much to use the computer but he simply couldn't remember the processes anymore. Straightforward things, opening a file and saving documents, just disappeared from his mind. His frustration was dreadful. I felt so sorry for him but also exasperated that he still kept at it. At first I tried to help him and show him how to do it, but you realize that it's never going to stick and you just have to give up and deter him from trying. That was really hard; we had some bad scenes, rows and arguments about that. I told him more than once that it was a choice between the computer and me!"

Colin raised his eyebrows at that and I smiled,

"I'm not sure that David took that in and he never believed me when I made threats!"

"I'm sure he didn't!"

"Now it's words and this really is tragic," I continued, determined, while I had Colin's ear, to say everything that was bottled up inside me. Colin didn't object.

"Quite frequently now he can't get even simple words right. I'll ask him to pass me the cup and he hands me a book. Or I'll say to put something on the table and he puts it on the chair." I sighed wearily before indulging my anger.

"How can this happen, Colin? How can someone who wrote poetry like his lose command of the simplest words?"

"It's cruel," Colin agreed. "And it's hard for you to watch it happening. Like Beethoven going deaf."

"What's more, at one moment I'm so sorry for him and the next he's driving me mad!"

"You're doing a great job," Colin tried to reassure me. "But to return to my question. Do you know why it happened?"

For a moment I failed to understand the question. Colin put the question again. "Does it run in families, a genetic thing?"

It was the question I never stopped asking myself.

"It can be that, sometimes," I told him. "In some cases it runs in families, but apparently not all that often. In David's family there is only one fairly distant instance of it. There appear to be several possible causes."

"Which are?"

"OK, apart from the inheritance factor there is actual physical damage to the brain. Boxers are one glaring example."

"But David was never a boxer, was he?"

"Never." I paused, for this was something I had often thought about. "I sometimes wonder...."

"What?" Colin prompted me.

"We'll never know, but once, when we were on our German posting, he took a terrible knock on the top of his head. We had one of those garage doors that go up and over and it fell on him and nearly knocked him out. It raised a great lump on his head."

"That's just one knock," Colin objected. "It's not like the constant hammering that boxers take."

"I know, but even so; I do wonder if it might have triggered something."

"What other causes are there?"

"Drug-taking. Youngsters experimenting with angel-dust in California in the Sixties developed these symptoms."

"But David...?"

"What do you know about what David was doing in the Sixties and Seventies? You were abroad then yourself. After he came back from Africa, marriage falling apart, I wonder quite a lot what was going on. In fact...."

My face must have shown my reluctance to broach the subject as Colin prompted me to continue, which I did in a rushed way.

"In fact, Colin, I wonder if David ever told me the half of it...." I paused again and then turned to face him squarely. "Don't people tell each other things when they get married? I used to think so; I must have been awfully naïve."

"Naïve? When you married David? Yes, I think you always were!"

I felt myself turning red with a combination of embarrassment and anger.

"That's so unkind of you!" I fumed at him "In any case, what can I do about it?"

"Nothing really," he replied soothingly. "Regard it rather as strength!" he suggested with a smile. And then, turning serious again, "But what has brought this on?"

"To be honest, Colin, at the moment I'm just so very, very angry with David, I find it difficult even to be kind. And that's not making the caring any easier. I'm not just angry with him – I'm angry with you, with all and any of his friends who stood by and didn't tell me anything."

"Hey, hang on! That's a bit hard!" he protested. "What are we supposed to have told you about?"

"I'll tell you," I replied.

If David had gone to the nursing home at the Summer Solstice it was nearer the Equinox, and certainly well into the autumn, when the manager summoned me. A review meeting had been scheduled at the Home to discuss how David was getting on, but already the murmurs coming from the nurses and the manager signalled that it wasn't looking good. The meeting at the Home was really too painful to recall: I had understood that for the first half David would not be there, but would be called in later on. For some reason I arrived after the meeting had started and, to my dismay, David was there, seated in the circle of staff and social workers. It was just too painful to hear him talked about in his presence, with sunken jaw and listless eyes and minimal comprehension of what was spoken, but nonetheless, as was painfully obvious to me, aware that it was all about him.

At first he had tried to behave as if this was one of his "meetings at the office". Then he had sunk into apathy, responding with little understanding when questions were addressed to him. All in all, I reflected, it had been the most disgraceful example of bureaucratic insensitivity that I could imagine. And it should not have been like that; if only I – or any one of them – had stood up and exposed the inappropriateness of having him there, then at least, without him, the rest of the meeting could have taken place in a frank atmosphere. Besides myself and David there had been the burly, hearty nurse, the one who had told me that when we met first I looked ready to cut my own throat, who took charge, the

Social Services care manager, a trainee care manager who was there for the experience and the nurse specialist.

In the end it was the Nursing Home manager who was saying that they could not keep David on a long-term basis, citing some evidence from his medical history, which somehow, apparently, made it unsuitable for him to stay. I had been so overcome by pity and guilt I said he should go home.

I left the meeting feeling I had done the right thing. The nursing home had not worked out and David would return home at the end of September.

Four days later I realized that I had just tied the noose around my neck again and sentenced myself, as it were, to who could tell how long of caring and being trapped, day and night, in my own home. My sons said I had done the wrong thing. We must give it longer at the Nursing Home, they insisted, and try to make it work.

More meetings were held and the Social Services care manager was helpful but doubted that the Nursing Home would reconsider. In particular there was something in David's medical records and I knew I had to get access to them to find out what the fuss was about.

I rang the doctor, the general practitioner, who attended at the nursing home several times and when I eventually got hold of him found that the voice on the end of the line was pleasant and quite relaxed about the idea of letting me see David's notes.

"It's not a problem. There may be something there which has worried the Home. Sometimes things from way back get exaggerated. You are welcome to read through the notes." He was going on holiday but would tell his secretary to make the notes available.

So, on a fine late summer afternoon I drove over to the surgery. The secretary had the notes ready and offered me the use of the doctor's consulting room since he was on holiday. I sat awkwardly at the doctor's spacious desk and opened the two buff folders, bulging with notes and letters leading back over years. Soon I forgot my surroundings as my thoughts were caught up by the material I was reading. For the next two hours, reading David's notes, I re-lived, year by year, the bad times, the months and years when they were searching for a diagnosis for whatever was afflicting him. There were notes from the neurological hospital in

London where he had gone for consultation while we were still overseas; there were notes of MRI-scans and mentions of vascular degeneration, there were references to the Mayo Clinic in the USA where he had gone for consultation whilst still in work, there were letters beginning "Dear Dr so and so, Thank you for sending me this very interesting patient". There were letters post-diagnosis, from the neurologist to David's doctor, including references to myself: "We try to support his wife who appears to be somewhat depressed...." I hated that bit: for God's sake, who would not be a bit depressed in that situation? But to suggest that I was clinically depressed because of a few tears shed in the consulting room was like an insult and a betrayal. I regarded myself almost a single-parent by then, attempting to be both father and mother, since David seemed to have given up the struggle to be role-model or mentor to his sons, I felt I coped pretty well. Wasn't the neurologist the person who was supposed to understand about this illness and all it entailed for families? And even though he wrote "We try to support his wife..." what had that actually amounted to?

I had seen that letter before and, although it temporarily revived my anger, I let it pass and moved on to the next folder. Here was something I hadn't seen before, two letters, dating from the early seventies. Hey, that was before I even knew David!

For the next forty minutes I read and was transfixed, reading, re-reading and taking down notes. So absorbed was I in what I found that the time passed unnoticed. I didn't have enough paper to write on, used backs of envelopes, the last page of a notebook, anything available and what I read was, to me, a revelation, letters apparently from a period when David had been in psychiatric care.

Why did I find this so shocking? For shocked was indeed how I felt.

I wanted to exclaim out loud. *Yes, yes, so that's what happened! That explains so much. That's a piece of the jig-saw. And why didn't I know about that? How could he have not mentioned that? And his friends? What were they doing? I asked myself. And what does this opinion passed from one medic to another mean?*

The two letters, which dated from before David and I had met, had somehow remained in his file along with all the more recent ones. With a strong feeling that I was committing an invasion of privacy I found myself drawn into a scene and a period of David's life from before I had known him. And I wasn't seeing the scene from David's point of view – had he ever seen these letters? – but through the eyes of the specialist and the language was that of the specialist to the civil servant. These letters provided some answers but they raised many more questions. I needed to know what was going on and whose voice was to be believed?

For forty minutes, in the quiet consulting room, I was carried back to the early Seventies, trying to fit the scenes that I was reading about, alongside my own memories of where I myself had been, in those days before I knew David, irrelevant though this might have been. There were personalities in these papers, people whom I would never meet or know or put my questions to but who, for forty minutes in this vacated doctor's space, were alive and real.

Two hours passed. I was due at the Nursing Home and the Surgery was closing. The receptionist came to tell me I must leave. I wondered if I should simply help myself to the letters which so interested me but decided against it and, with as much as I could manage copied onto scraps of paper and folded into my handbag, I handed the package back to the receptionist, and from the dim corridors of the early nineteen seventies, walked out into a late afternoon of the early twenty-first century.

"And so you see, Colin," I told him, "Since then, since learning all that, I've been speculating. What really happened to David, that year after he came back from Nigeria, in London? What was the truth of it? And why didn't he tell me about that episode?"

"Would it have made much difference if he had?" Colin asked.

I left the question unanswered: I had to think about it.

And as I think about it, much, much later, I can understand, a little more clearly, how that news affected me. The answer to Colin's question might have been either way. I hope it would not have made a difference but it would have given me a better understanding of the complex person I was about to join my life with, which might have made me more able to cope. As it was, did he not trust me with that piece of history? And what else did he not trust me with? I felt like saying "*You could have told me*!" And then I asked myself – "*But could he?*"

WHITE CORRIDORS

The Lovers
DO YOU LOVE YOUR WIFE?
An equation without
Constants cannot be resolved.
DO? Actions root
And snuffle circumstance
YOU? I am a singular
Plurality   Reduce me
LOVE? The Mallory perhaps
Time swallows us   We
Never do come back
The mountain malady remains
YOUR? Property is theft
Thereby implying ownership
WIFE? Machines for living in
Give up the ghost   Enlarge her

YOU ARE NOT PLAYING THE GAME

No. The game is not playing me.

September 2004
Days — which ran into weeks — passed as I read and re-read the
notes I had made of those two letters, trying to work out what the
contents referred to, looking up words in medical dictionaries and
on the internet and attempting to work out what relevance any of it
might have had to our relationship and to David's present state of
health. The letters were headed with the address of a hospital in
North London and it was there, I reckoned, that things had come to
a head.

North London, 1972
Long corridors looked out onto extensive grounds: grass and cedar
trees, white wards, cubicled beds, laundry-faded bed-covers. On a
day bright with spells of sunshine, the effect was nonetheless

chilling. David had been here too long: now the nurse had come for him.

"Dr Barnet is here, David. He'll see you in the room next to the Matron's office."

He heaved himself reluctantly off the bed. His face was gaunt, the curly hair lank, his face untanned. Pocketing the pack of Marlboroughs from the bedside table, patting his pockets to ensure he had matches, keeping a defiant distance behind her, he followed the nurse. Their footsteps echoed on the polished floor, the length of the corridor. Some patients looked up as they passed, others remained slumped in chairs, one was talking to the door-post.

Holding the office door open, the nurse let David pass through. Dr Barnet, Consultant Psychiatrist, got up from the desk and lent across to offer a handshake. He was wearing his white coat – predictably, thought David, it's a badge of office, a symbol of power. Well, the power would not go unchallenged. He ignored the handshake and slumped into the chair, stretching his legs and crossing his ankles. Uninvited he lit a cigarette, shook the match out, looked conspicuously for an ash tray and, finding none, ostentatiously replaced the used match in the box. His gaze challenged the man opposite him, who enquired mildly,

"How are we feeling today?"

"*We*?" David queried. "*We*? If you insist on the plural form, *we* are feeling fine and we don't need to be here. We are probably taking up space needed by others who have real problems," David told him and continued at an increasing pace, "God, when I think of the number of people who need your attention, you're wasting tax-payers' money, to say the least of it, by insisting that I stay in this….."

"Mr Handley," the doctor was unruffled by the challenge and continued in the same mild tone, "You are in here simply for observation and to see if we can decide on a course of treatment."

David snorted.

"The aim is to restore your calm and, erm, how shall I put it? Perhaps 'a clear state of mind' sums it up."

"I don't have any problem with my state of mind, thank you! My state of mind is one of creative activity, continually, both in my work and in my own time. If you are trying to dampen down my creative instincts, that sounds suspiciously to me like the state harnessing the power of the medical establishment; silencing dissent from the public discourse of the day: is that your agenda?. To silence the voices which articulate meanings for our times? In other words – the Gulag."

There was a pause. The doctor appeared to reflect on David's outburst, and although he was nodding and observing his patient's demeanour, it was not apparent that he had taken much interest in what had been said:

"My aim," he began, then corrected himself, "I should say *our* aim ... our aim is to arrive at a course of treatment for the condition which has been diagnosed: treatment which will allow you to return to your work. And to your wife...." He paused again and looked enquiringly at David, "If, in fact, that is what she and you wish. And to put this episode behind you once and for all." He smiled encouragingly.

"Ah! 'Once and for all'," David grabbed at the expression. "We could take that phrase and analyse it in terms of the pragmatics of the situation; now that would be interesting!" He paused. "But first, this diagnosis that you mention. 'Diagnosis' being a proposition, and apparently an objective one, requiring a subject, which presumably is the role I fill, then if I'm to avoid being 'positioned as the subject' into a space which I certainly wouldn't wish to occupy...." He paused for breath, then, searching for the thread of his discourse and finding it, continued, "Since I am the 'subject' at the centre of this discourse then I'm entitled to know what diagnosis has been made, and to let you know if I agree with it: isn't that so? That would be the 'collaborative methodology' wouldn't it? So let's hear your diagnosis – Doctor!"

The doctor responded quietly. "The diagnosis is one of hypomania. Possible personality disorder is ...."

He was interrupted by an explosive eruption as David rose and reached across the desk to snatch the paper that Dr Barnet was reading from. The doctor pulled back, preventing him from taking the papers. His patience was running short now. "Unfortunately I'm not able to take into account your agreement or non-agreement. Unfortunately – and I really am unable to phrase this in any other way – but your opinion is not relevant. The diagnosis is within the province of the specialist and not the layman. I hope you can understand my point of view."

"Even if the layman is the person being diagnosed upon? Incredible. But what, just what is a 'diagnosis'? 'Words, words!' And signifying nothing!"

The psychiatrist attempted a smile but it was becoming ever more forced. "It's always enjoyable when a consultation provides the opportunity for sharing literary allusions but we must not be side-tracked. In this case it is the responsibility of the specialist to prescribe the treatment for the condition. I'd like to start you on Lithium Carbonate and to see you here again in two weeks time. Meantime, Mr Handley, you'll be well-cared for. You stay put and rest up."

"Just two points there *Mister* Barton," David was up for the challenge now, but decided to goad his opponent first. "It strikes me as strange that as soon as you doctors become elevated to the higher ranks, you immediately demote yourself! Why the Mr? I've always wondered about it and conclude that it's your own form of inverted snobbery."

"Could be, but I *am* a doctor. Put it down to tradition."

"Ah, which of us would have got where we are without tradition?" David mused. "For my own part I would probably still be here, but the good doctors...."

Dr Barton was writing on a prescription pad:

"This will be dispensed today and we'll start you on it this evening. Was there anything else? What were your two points?"

"David sat up straight. "OK. Point one is simply this. I don't take your petro-chemical drug prescriptions and point two: I don't 'stay put' here. As far as I'm concerned, that's it; ... had enough ... I'm off." He stood up and turned for the door.

"Not 'off', Mr Handley. Regrettably you are here under an Order."

"Regrettably! Everything seems to be 'regrettable' in your view! And the status of this so-called 'Order'? And by whose orders am I under this 'Order'?"

"Your wife, Mr Handley, applied for the Order in view of your disturbed behaviour over the last six to nine months. We've been over it before." He sighed wearily. "It's a Court Order. You are free to leave the hospital and grounds for short periods during the day, provided you give notice of where you are going, and provided also that you do not go near your wife. Nevertheless you are bound by the Order to remain resident within the hospital and follow the full course of prescribed treatment."

David turned from the door to the desk, seating himself with a leg hitched over the corner of the desk, at an angle and in close proximity to the white-coated consultant. For all his defiance, his face was drawn and haggard.

Barnet continued: "Lithium Carbonate" is commonly used in the treatment of hypomania, for the illness you are suffering from…"

"I am not suffering from any illness! And I am especially not suffering from hypomania! I have told you this before."

"It is your wife's opinion that you are indeed suffering from such an illness…."

"Well, she would say that, wouldn't she?"

"Your wife has described to me in careful detail the changes she has noted in your behaviour…"

"And she has charmed you and twisted you round her little finger. Isn't that exactly the case? Surrounded by the frumpy set of nurses which we see in this place it's hardly surprising that someone like her would have you eating out of her hand."

The doctor shrugged dismissively.

"Just watch it! That's all I say, and don't think I'm prepared to take any of your mind-altering chemicals, thank you! I've said it before; homeopathic medication is the only routine I'll accept. You can put your drugs…you know where."

"Mr Handley" – the doctor made a visible effort to regain a calm tone of voice – "Your wife's description of behavioural changes and my own observations leave no room for doubt that your condition is one of hypomania." The effort was becoming too much and he added with some force, "Indeed your exalted state and extreme loquaciousness are further confirmation. If any were needed."

"You know, the trouble with you shrinks," David began. – It was a cheap jibe and he saw the psychiatrist wince. – "The trouble with you lot is that you're always one-up on the rest of us." He knew he was being gratuitously insulting and the sensation was going to his head. Stay cool, he reminded himself. This guy's got the upper hand on you. Pin-pricks are all you can give, but keep at it! "As soon as we lay-victims explain ourselves, back you come with another trick from up your sleeve."

"I do my best to understand your point of view, Mr Handley, to listen to what you say. I'm treating you under a Court Order and it's wrong to think I'm simply trying to trump anything you have to say. In fact it's completely counter-productive!"

David noticed the way he was re-arranging the items on the desk and glancing at the clock on the wall; he clearly wanted to bring the interview to an end: keep going, he told himself, but change the pace.

"Let's keep this calm, shall we?" David suggested. "Just relax. Don't get excited." He could see the doctor biting back his irritation. It was a moment to take advantage of. "Let's discuss the pros and cons, the fors and againsts if you prefer, of the drug régime that you want to put me on."

The doctor sighed. "Mr Handley, we've been over the ground time and again. You have self-prescribed for yourself," he looked at his notes, "a régime of St John's Wort with steam baths and massage sessions. I, on the other hand, as the specialist, am prescribing Lithium Carbonate. It would be unnecessary for me to remind you of my specialist training and years of psychiatric practice, of the clinical panels and panels of medical ethics that I serve on. All that would try your patience. Simply believe me when I say that what I'm prescribing for you is a treatment which will restore you to a state of mind in which you will be able to continue with your career." His tone was increasingly persuasive. "I am assured by many that you are highly respected in your work. All that is needed is for you to return to a state of mind in which you will be able to continue that work and contemplate with detachment and rationality, the future or otherwise of your marriage to your very attractive wife."

But David was having none of it. "Ha! I knew she'd trapped you! And No, No, and No. It's St John's Wort or nothing and none of your mind-bending chemical medications. *I don't do drugs*!"

Dr Barton looked curiously at him. "You don't do drugs. Are you sure about that?"

"Certainly not your kind of drugs!"

"But possibly some other kinds. The kind that everyone in the..." – He searched for a phrase." – the artistic world is doing? After all, perhaps we should explore that line?"

"The artistic world?" David enquired. "Sure, why not. Do you happen to know anything about the artistic world? I mean, I don't suppose you get much time for that sort of thing – with so many medical panels and committees to attend?"

"I do understand from your wife that you spend time at the home of poets and writers: the foremost of the group being, I understand, a gentleman from the Indian sub-continent."

"And so...? Have I missed out on something? Has that become a crime? And is it the associating with poets and writers, or the associating with gentlemen from the Indian sub-continent which is the particular crime? Don't forget that we have had the Race Relations Act for some time now..."

"Mr Handley, it isn't helpful to be on the defensive. And it isn't helpful to be ironic either. In your wife's view you spend far more time after work at this writers' circle than you do with her..."

"For Christ's sake, she could come too; she could always come, but she chooses not to!"

"And much time also at an artistic commune modelled on the lines of a San Francisco drop-out centre where you do...." He consulted his notes again and quoted from them. "', , , Jackson Pollock-style murals?'"

"What would you know about Jackson Pollack-style murals? Although I can tell you that in California art therapy is Big!"

".... and that you come home in the early hours, and not a little intoxicated."

"With tea! We drink tea. Nothing stronger!"

"Tea certainly is not an intoxicant and I know as well as you do that drinking isn't the only route to...."

"Heightened experience? Is that what you are on about? Magic mushrooms? It's an interesting subject. More common in Central America than the Indian Sub-continent."

"You're quite well-informed, which I can take as an indication...."

"An indication of what? Anyone with more than a passing interest in contemporary art, music, poetry, knows as much as I do. Certainly in your profession I'd have thought....

"Have thought what?"

David paused before responding, sensing a topic which he would dearly love to discuss, at the same time finding a need for caution.

"Carlos Castaneda? Aldous Huxley and "The Gates of Perception", you must have read that?

"Indeed, I've looked at it. The writer comes at his subject from an angle which is the opposite of my own of course...Still, from your own experience, would you say that the effects he describes are authentic?"

There it was: the trap set! Well, he wasn't walking into it.

"How could I say?" David replied. "But there's evidence all around you, isn't there? If you use your ears? And your imagination. Picture yourself, I mean..." He hummed a tune. "'Picture yourself in a boat on a river.' How does it go on? Something about Lucy? ... Sky? ... Diamonds? ... Everyone's humming it."

The doctor smiled.

David continued, "Then there's colours. 'Psychedelic' is the word! Look at fashions! Though you'd have to get out of the Hospital of course. Get away from the white coats and the nurses' uniforms. Go and sit by the statue of Eros for ten minutes, if you want psychedelic colours and patterns. On the other hand, if you spend your life between the Hospital and the suburbs, the evidence of psychedelic activity would be easy to miss altogether."

The doctor made notes, paused, and looked up.

"Clearly you haven't missed much and you lead a fascinating existence. Would you perhaps describe yourself as deeply immersed in the experience of heightened awareness?"

David countered quickly. "I describe myself as being deeply immersed in contemporary culture but I've no wish to end up in the dock or put my job on the line and I would not describe myself as being deeply immersed in the drug scene, if that is what you're trying to say. I've got more sense than that!"

And with this deeply ambiguous statement, Mr Barton had to be content, for next thing he knew David had reached across and whipped up the note book in which the doctor had been writing.

Scanning the page he took out a pen and scored deep lines through the last paragraph inserting his own words in their place and enunciating as he did so.

"'*Mr Handley tells me that he is deeply immersed in contemporary culture.* – Full stop!' What shall we talk about next? I'd like to discuss the Kabbalah: are you up to it?"

But the psychiatrist had had enough. Glancing at his watch he signalled that his time was up.

"The Kabbalah will have to wait for another day. Mr Handley, I'm here to help you. Your condition is a cause for concern, to your wife, your friends, your employers, and not least to the Senior Medical Officer of the Civil Service, to whom I have to submit a report to at the end of your treatment. You can probably see the implications of the last of these. The nurse will give you the medication after your meal this evening and I want to urge you to persevere with it. There may be side-effects to start with, but they'll pass."

He stood and held out his hand. This time David took it. They parted, not entirely on bad terms.

"It's been interesting talking, doctor. See you!"

David picked up his cigarettes and, brushing past the nurse who was waiting to enter, left without looking back.

Three days later Dr Barton received two friends of David. Colin was one of them and another colleague had taken time off and walked the few streets from the Organisation's offices to Dr Barton's address in Wigmore Street. They were soberly suited, as indeed they always were for the office, and could have been any Whitehall Civil Servants – except perhaps for something in the demeanour and the challenging look in their eyes. The conversation took place in the psychiatrist's office.

"Tell us exactly what 'hypomania' signifies, if you would," Colin asked.

"It's used to describe a state of over-arousal and excitability with persistently elevated mood, often accompanied by undue irritability and intolerance of others. I find that this is an accurate description of your friend's illness."

"Are you sure that it is an illness?" the second friend asked. "I mean, David is like that a lot of the time. It's why he's so good at his job."

"Often it's accompanied by hyper-sexuality and social disinhibition and sometimes even delusions of grandeur."

"David does not suffer from delusions of grandeur." Colin challenged him. "But he does have ambitions. It's not the same thing at all. Personally I would not say he was ill and I'm sorry that he has been made to stay in hospital. In fact it's very distressing indeed."

"Yes, you may say that. But I have to take into consideration the reports from his wife," the doctor responded, "And the distress he has been causing her. In fact," he continued, "I can't see that she could maintain her own equilibrium for much longer if he isn't treated."

"Ah, but there you have it!" Colin cut in. "She doesn't understand him. She's not on his wave-length and never has been! Dr Barton." Colin leaned forward, compelling the doctor to meet his gaze. "In my view David is close to being a genius." Then, noting the sceptical expression on the doctor's face, "No! Listen; I believe that. And that's something she can't understand or cope with."

"Hmm, I grant you his intelligence," the doctor responded, "But genius? In which respect, would you say?" he enquired.

"Actually it would be hard to explain.... No disrespect, of course."

The doctor raised his eyebrows and paused for several seconds before replying.

"Passing on from that then, why, in your view, did he marry her?"

"Or she him...we should add," the colleague spoke up. "It takes two after all."

Colin glanced at his companion and continued, "David married Sugar – that's what he calls her – out of pure romance, in my view. She was beautiful, a lonely dancer, struggling. He had high pretensions in the artistic field. He got carried away by the idea of it all. He didn't know what marriage was about. And as everyone knows who works with him, his enthusiasm is hard to resist. If he had decided they were going to get married, she'd have found it hard to resist him. Once he has a project underway, everyone gets caught up in the excitement."

The doctor nodded reflectively. "Yes, I can see that."

"The difference is," Colin continued, "That with his work, the projects are usually well-based in reality. David has a talent for spotting what will work and for putting the right people in the right places and then letting them get on with it. But in his personal life it's not so good. The marriage has never worked. She hates all his off-the-wall artistic and poetical ideals. She would like a more conventional life.

"She led him a bad dance in Africa, took lovers when she thought it might help her personal career and so forth. That took him completely by surprise and wounded him."

The doctor was thoughtful. "His wife assures me that he has been in a hypo-manic state for six months now."

"She wants out! That's why she got you to lock him up!"

"I must insist!" The doctor was offended. "Locking people up is not something I do. A Court Order was made and as a result I have been seeing this gentleman – your friend and colleague – and attempting to do my best for him.… And for his wife."

"Just be careful of the wife – that's all I say," Colin warned. "Though on the whole I'd say they would be best apart. He'll never let go without something like this, so perhaps she's just taken the only way out."

"I have a report to write, which is why I asked you to come here. So, in your opinion, your friend is not acting unduly out of character?"

"On the whole I should say no. Maybe just a bit excessive in recent weeks, but that is probably down to the publishing project."

The doctor looked enquiring.

"Did you not know about that? He's taken on a lot by offering to raise funds for a poetry publication. It's the Lyrebird Press: nothing to do with his regular work. They're bringing out an anthology of London verse. That's what has been taking up so much of his time, plus, of course, his job, where he is also overloaded and short-staffed."

"And would the publishing account for the large overdraft on their joint bank account? You see, one of his wife's problems is that he not only neglects her but also leaves her short of funds and, indeed has drawn on funds –from their joint account – which come from her own earnings."

"Definitely! He can sometimes be a bit reckless where money is concerned. When funds are needed for a project, he finds it wherever he can: his bank account, hers, an overdraft….In his view it shouldn't matter, because the concern for him is getting the project completed."

The doctor reflected on these words before resuming.

"Thank you both, I'm grateful for your opinion. The trouble with such illnesses is that the patients are notoriously difficult to treat, and the more intelligent they are, the more havoc they can wreak both on others and themselves."

David and Dr Barton were seated once again in the office next to the Matron's.

"I'm not going to oblige you to stay here any longer Mr Handley. The Order expires today and you have been following the treatment I prescribed and I cannot in all honesty say that you are sufficiently ill to warrant me applying for a further Order under Section 26 of the Mental Health Act. However, I do strongly advise you to remain and continue the treatment under supervision and to benefit from the surroundings and calm atmosphere."

"Section 26?" David looked startled, "You can't mean what I think you mean?"

The doctor raised enquiring eyebrows but, as David stayed silent, he proceeded with what he had to say. "You should continue, in all cases, with the prescribed medication…"

David interrupted him. "Medication is for illness and I've never admitted to having any illness other than the normal coughs and colds. Now, if you have anything that I can take away to guard against the flu – fair enough, otherwise…"

"Mental illness is not always so easily…"

"The concept of mental illness, as I've said before, is all too often used as a tool of repression. And that being the case I find it hard to believe in the psychiatrists' so-called treatments for an invented illness."

The doctor sighed wearily, not for the first time.

"I'm at least glad that you are less irritable and argumentative than at our last meeting. However, frankly, I do not feel strong enough to argue the minutiae of cellular biochemistry with you. I understand that your employers have agreed for you to take some time off work, and I think this is an excellent idea. I feel sure you will come out of this illness fairly soon and I think it would be a great pity if you were to lose your job in these circumstances. I shall make this point in my letter to the Senior Medical Officer at the Civil Service Department. I trust you will be happy with this. No doubt others will make their own minds up when you are back to normal ... whatever 'normal' may be," he added, shaking his head slightly, "in your particular case".

David was, undoubtedly, heartily relieved, but had the diplomacy to look grateful.

"The nurse will ensure that you have sufficient supplies of the medication and I strongly advise you to continue the treatment."

"Thanks, doc. I'll certainly think about taking it regularly. I can see that I may have been acting a bit theatrically."

"Theatrically...?" the doctor echoed, enquiringly. "You will not be continuing with the publishing, I presume?"

"Most certainly! It has to go ahead. My wife needn't worry. The money will be on loan from the bank."

"Your wife insists that the overdraft be paid off. Beyond that she has no concerns. She has set up her own flat, I understand, and wishes not to communicate."

It was a sad note to end on. Both men stood, shook hands. David left the room.

I stopped speaking and sat for a moment, staring into my own inner space, then turned to Colin.

"Maybe that's how it was, Colin. I'm surmising of course, trying to piece together something from the clues I've been given and to see how I feel about it. Anyway, I know how you stood by him and I'm grateful for that – as I'm sure he was – if he ever knew?"

I ended on a question, but Colin only smiled.

After a pause, both of us deep in thought, I continued.

"I know I've asked this before, but don't people tell each other such things when they get married?"

Colin smiled, sympathetically, but with a shake of his head and a gesture, which showed his reservations on the subject.

There was a pause while I remembered how this conversation had started, then I continued. "To go right back to that question you asked, 'Why did this disease happen to David?' Don't you think maybe it was drugs in the seventies, the cause of how he is now?"

Colin sighed. "A remote chance, I should say. We neither of us really know what he got up to in that respect. Same as the blow on the head. We won't ever know."

THE DYING OF THE YEAR

Prayers
thirty nine
three covens of you
three circlings of the years
about three crumpling continents
& today
on the spiral's axis
as we two
lean into one twisting future
may we love
being into being

let there be
a slow cauldron of calm
let the days
that crackle & splutter beneath it
be worlds we spoke
& let the figures
achant on its rim
their thumbs and little fingers throbbing
be wild
in red eyed grace

in your own spaces
let the wind fetch
clean clouds
that you may stay
gentle

December 2004
David still enjoyed an outing to the pub at lunch time and New
Year's Eve had to be a special occasion. We set off for the Buck's
Head and arrived soon after mid-day. The landlord knew us and
understood David's difficult speech.
    "P-p-p-pint of best bitter."

"And the same for me," I added. "And a packet of cheese and onion." I anticipated David's request.

"I'll carry that," I said, indicating the glass but David had got there first and, after taking a good sip was making his way unsteadily towards a table. I held my breath; the landlord did the same but David made it safely – once more I marvelled at how, unsteady as he was, given a glass in his hand, he seldom spilled a drop!

Enjoying the warmth and the buzz of conversation around us, David didn't feel the need to talk and that was just as well, since talking at the same time as eating or drinking was out of the question. We ordered our plaice and chips with peas and sat back to enjoy the atmosphere. Seeing David so relaxed and happy in his familiar surroundings was bitter-sweet: I looked forward with dread to what must be continued, slow, decline. How could I prevent the thought that it would be better for him to "leave now", while he was happy and contented despite the terrible change in his circumstances, rather than go through who knew what indignities, loss, and suffering of a slow, downward spiral?

That was a feeling that I later came to revise when, despite the enormity of the changes that had taken place, I realised that there continued to be moments of contentment and enjoyment in his life. It's a difficult lesson and, as we sat together in the pub, I was very far from appreciating it. Seeing David enjoying the buzz of conversation and the cheerful atmosphere, I could not help thinking that this would be a good point for him to make his exit. Guiltily I banished the thought. David was trying to ask me something and having difficulty finding the words. Curiously, while easy, everyday words and phrases frequently eluded him, the poetical ones came readily to his tongue. I could see him looking at the decorations and the festive scene and casting around:

"Is it….?" he paused, searching.

"Is it…?" I prompted…

"Is it the dying of the year?"

Of course! That was what he wanted to know. "Yes, that's right! It's New Year's Eve!"

He smiled, pleased, and turned to his food only to encounter another difficulty. Sometimes objects in front of his eyes could not be seen; he wanted the fork, but could find neither the object nor the word.

"Do we have a ...?"

"Do we have a...? What do you need?" I prompted.

"A three-pronged..." He cast about again for the word. "...A three-pronged trident?"

"A fork; there it is." I handed it to him. All was well.

It was curious how the power of speech had become so impaired. The psychiatrist had drawn diagrams of different parts of the brain, in an attempt to show how different functions were affected. David seemed to lose the simplest of words, whilst retaining others, which were, frankly, esoteric. He smiled when I pointed out to him that, when he couldn't find a word, he reverted to poetry. He must have felt it proved his point!

We spent the afternoon quietly at the house. David snoozed by the fire but woke when I came in with tea.

"Shall we have some poems?" I proposed, and he nodded, pleased. It was not every day that I had the time or the inclination to sit quietly with him like this, and read outloud. I chose several, ending up with one of his own, written for me several years before, when the children were small, celebrating my birthday. Should those lines be taken as irony? Certainly none was intended at the time. On the other hand that "slow cauldron of calm" that David invoked in 'Prayers', the poem he had written for my thirty-ninth birthday: yes, there were moments, like these, when we achieved it.

At 5.30 I gave David his supper, pâté and toast, followed by a dessert and ice-cream. After that he disappeared to his room, and I went to have a bath and wash my hair.

When I came down, feeling somewhat guilty at having left him for so long, to my dismay, I found the kitchen in a mess but no sign of David. He had helped himself to more food and a mess of mashed bananas adorned the kitchen worktop and a ripe pear had been cut up and was distributed at various points between the kitchen, dining room, sitting room and bedroom. I followed the trail. David was in his bathroom, stuck. He had lost his mobility and I realised with a guilty start that I had forgotten the tablets at six o'clock. I found him in some distress and administered a "rescue tablet" along with the overdue six o'clock regular one.

Unable to move, he was also unable to speak. But the situation was clear. Having got up off the loo, he had frozen; he was wearing just a shirt, with only one sleeve on correctly, the underpants were on the floor and he rocked unsteadily from side to side as I quickly fetched the wheelchair and steadied him, noticing again how painfully thin his legs were. Having come back from the Nursing Home as thin as a skeleton – they said it was because he was so restless and walked around the entire time – he was now putting on a bit of weight. Nevertheless, his legs were like sticks. The bones of his buttocks stuck out, with their cracked skin. His belly was pot-bloated where the needle of the syringe was stuck into it and the tube carrying the medication from the little pump in his breast pocket, protruded. This was a moment for gentleness and not the ironic remarks, which occasionally sprang, unwanted, to my lips. I helped him through from bathroom to the bedroom.

"Let's get your shirt straight, shall we?" I eased his other arm into its sleeve. "Now, here are your pants. Lift this leg." I directed and helped each movement. "Good, now the other one; well done!" We were nearly there. "Here's the wheel-chair, now let's get you some pyjama trousers. That's better."

My running commentary accompanied the sequence of movements, compensating for the fact that David could not get any speech out. I got him to bed, where he lay back gratefully, brought him something to drink and set the television to a suitable channel.

Sitting at the kitchen table I poured the last of a bottle of red wine into a glass and put the empty bottle outside the back door. Then, on second thoughts I picked it up and took it to the shed to put with others ready for the bottle bank next day. The carer was coming in the morning and I didn't want to complicate things by letting her think I had a drinking problem. I took my glass through to the sitting room and collapsed into an armchair in front of the television. I hoped that David was settled and would sleep for a bit, or at least doze now. It was just gone eight in the evening. Most probably he would be awake at 10.30 or 11pm. Often when I went to give him his overnight tablets I found him dressed for the morning. Then the whole undressing, putting on pyjamas, getting to the bathroom and back to bed had to be done over again. Being so sedentary meant that sores on his bottom were making life even more difficult. At night he was unable to move onto his side or front, so his "b-t-m" as it was playfully referred to, got no relief at all and either I or the carer had to spread the yellow, sticky cream over the scabs and cracks. The tube containing the ointment had a picture of a smiling baby, kicking its feet in the air while its mother held its ankles and patted its bottom.

At eight pm I probably had a couple of hours to wind down. Maybe I would open another bottle of wine. In other times I might have been going out – singing in a choir had been one regular activity, attending school meetings, parish council – and before that – it seemed so long ago that I could hardly remember it – we had actually gone out together. That was then; but now there was no possibility of a social life and in any case I was generally too tired to start on anything more enterprising than reading the paper and searching for something to watch on the television.

I was becoming addicted to certain programmes and finding that they dictated the evenings for me. Tonight there was a new detective serial episode to watch on TV; could be entertaining. More wine? Don't mind if I do!

Although I put the bottles out of sight, I wasn't ashamed of myself. It was the way I managed to cope with the situation. I had tried to escape, but the nursing home had been a flop. So, since everyone said I had to cope, that was one way to do it. And anyway, I knew I could cut it back when – if – the situation ever changed, if it was ever over. Meanwhile, just make the best of things, and a glass of wine certainly helped.

One way or another I coped and in fact, I suspected I was probably better off than many who didn't get the help that I did. Employing a carer to look after David from nine to five every day was what made it possible. I was able to get out and carry on my new and struggling business in the town. It gave me a life and having to fight to get the business off the ground was certainly a distraction from the slow grind and the endless calls on my patience of looking after David. When I got back in the evenings, the carer had usually got his supper ready, so I had only to give it to him. The carer was a treasure and I didn't know how she managed the long days. I was really very lucky.

Later that night, "Fuck, fuck, fuck, fuck, fuck, fuck, buggering hell." The words held a certain rhythm and I repeated them as I rushed from his bedroom to fetch a wet cloth from the kitchen.

"Why can't you make a bit of an effort, David? Why don't you try, at least?"

As I suspected, David had got up and got dressed when I had dozed off in front of the television and I had to get him back to bed. Once again we went through the slow process of one careful movement after another, changing his trousers for pyjamas, helping him to perch on the side of the bed, getting him to swing his legs up and onto the bed and then, after minute instruction to press his two hands down and lift himself up and across into the middle of the bed. My patience was wearing thin.

"Anything else required?" I enquired wearily.

"The Shakespeare book..."

It was on the bedside table, beside the glass of juice, out of my reach.

"Make an effort David, you can reach it!" My back was aching abominably. Somehow, at this late stage of the evening I rebelled at making the effort on his behalf.

With dreadful deliberation he inched his hand towards it.

"Don't make such a drama of it! Just pick it up!" I felt like saying. He must be able to do better than this! This was a performance put on just to annoy me!

Slowly, David got hold of the book and lifted it by one corner; the cover flapped downward towards the glass of juice; the tipping and the spilling were inevitable.

Clamping my mouth shut I made for the kitchen: "Fuck, fuck, fuck, fuck, fuck, fuck, buggering hell!" I chanted in silent fury through my teeth. Not that it helped a lot; back in the bedroom with my cloth I pounded the sticky yellow pool on the carpet – just one of many other stains, some far less wholesome in origin. Why had I bothered to have the carpet chemically cleaned three weeks ago? Now it reeked!

I mopped up the residues on the table: switched on a smile.

"That's it; all done! See you in a bit!" I retired to the television, to sigh and pour myself a glass of wine. Was this what you called life?

"Why didn't you warn me?" I had asked Colin.

"What about?" he replied.

"Before we were married, didn't you know the kind of life David had been leading?"

I had thought that Colin was my friend as well as David's.

And he had told me; it was he who had spoken of Genius.

"That time he returned home," Colin told me, "on leave from Iran, he told me about you. You see, he had this girl-friend here in London, Joanna. She had Hungarian connections, which was somewhat exotic, and I think they planned to get married, except that Joanna was not at all keen on going to Iran. Then he met you! You had this good, homely, secure, middle-class appeal. And that was his dilemma: he wasn't sure which of you he should marry."

I raised my eyebrows. "It was as simple as that?"

"I just told him what I thought he should do."

"So it was like..." I reflected for a moment. "Like tossing a coin, was it? .... Me or Joanna. Which should it be?"

"Oh come on – don't be ridiculous." Colin was irritated now. "David needed stability. He needed someone to anchor all that brilliance. You were what he needed! And in any case he probably wouldn't have listened to my advice, if he hadn't agreed with it all along."

My mind jumped back to those early days after David and I had met in Tehran. No home leave was due to me and I had worked the whole summer in the sweltering city heat, while David had returned to London, leaving me in suspense.

I remembered the time, vividly, but preferred not to recall it in detail. To me the month when David had been away on leave had been a time to hold my breath: would he come back engaged? I didn't know for sure if I was in love with him – in some ways it seemed more urgent than that – and I had not dared to contemplate the alternative. Together David and I would do great things. The plan had been China, the rising star in the Organisation's map of the universe. Together we would be posted to China; see great sights and do great things; that was the future.

And when David came back from London he was still not committed, still available.

We were becoming what would now be called an item but I could summon up no romantic memory of a first kiss.

One memory did come back to me: a meeting in David's office, sitting with others round a table. A phone-call interrupted the flow and he went to the desk to take it. Listening with one ear I could sense tension, embarrassment and David unusually at a loss for words. He brought the call to an end and put the phone down firmly. The moment passed and the meeting resumed but David told me later that it was Joanna on the other end of the phone, calling in some desperation from London. That signalled his moment of decision, and from then on we started to make plans together.

Where my family was concerned David was still defiantly wondering what he was getting himself into. In our working life your background and where you came from was an irrelevance and my close middle-class family remained in the background. Although I had given it little thought it went without saying that my parents would want to welcome a son-in-law into the circle and I now felt some wariness in David.

"Is your father an old fogey?" he asked.

I was shocked. How could he imagine that!

"Of course not! But my parents would like to do a wedding; they've been longing for that."

"I'll write to your father, but not to ask his permission!"

"I don't think he would even expect you to," I replied. David showed me the letter which he wrote and it was charming – and, I reflected, he had such beautiful handwriting in those days.

We seemed to spend hours making plans. China was just part of them. We shared the spirit of adventure and a belief in the aims of the Organisation we worked for. Sometimes I thought that this partnership was perhaps just too businesslike, a coincidence of self-interests; he wanted the stability that I offered, I wanted the future that he offered, a chance for a family, a husband with an assured career with postings around the world; was this alliance just one of supreme convenience? Perhaps we both felt that way until one night making love we shared a moment of such deep tenderness that it took the two of us by surprise; we voiced the same thought – this was something which seemed to set the seal of approval on our designs.

Nevertheless, in the middle of being carried away, I was aware of intimations of frailty in David. These also I pushed aside, to be dealt with later. Later, when the time came, I would cope with whatever they signified.

"He'll need a cushion," I thought. "That's what I might end up being –a cushion."

In some undefined way I had foreseen it in abstract and had risked it, telling myself – not in words –it never got that high in my consciousness –but subconsciously, certainly, "I won't be trapped: I'll deal with it firmly, when the time comes."

All the same, I had taken the risk; and I still hadn't entirely worked out to my own satisfaction, why.

Trapped and frustrated in the role of carer and unable to fulfil any wider ambitions, I was finding out now what that early sensation had signified.

To divert these black thoughts, I turned again to David's poem that I had read to him earlier, and it brought tears to my eyes. Our children, the "figures a-chant on the rim" had brought us so much joy – those dreams had come true – but as for the rest of it, David's prayer for me:

In your own spaces
Let the wind fetch
Clean clouds
That you may stay gentle.

No, I felt, that was not at all what I had become. That could not be further from the truth.

Exhausted by the thoughts churning in my head, I switched on the television again. It was only the news, murder and mayhem in the Middle East. The year was ending. But I felt that the poisonous mixture of grief and anger, which was infecting me like an illness, would never end.

SWITCHING ROLES

Holly Bush Lane
Coach House, 7 Holly Bush Lane.
Blue and white Aegean frontage.
Hanging boxes of geranium.
Hedge of rowanberry, lilac, pine, entwined.
Just recently hacked back, thinned, splintered.
Glimpses of hockey, soccer.

The warning symbols spring-buried in the hedge
are visible again. The red triangle alarm. The legend
elderly people. The bent spine age images in the icon.

Inside the red triangle sign, two figures stain
the pavement, their shadows almost standing up,
an elderly male stooping on his stick,
an elderly woman following, clutching his coat tails,
his journey hers.

Dr Parkinson I presume? And your gallery
of slow, glacially slow, characters.
the utter eerie peace. Patience on a monument. Sheer stasis.

I bring you spasms and paralysis in broken language
stuttering locked into spluttering syllables.
You talk of dopamine, acetylcholine
messengers of control of movement.
A shortage of these stiffens muscles,
mineralises them, delivers motion slow as
glistering slugs, tremors on lips and hands,
blurred double vision...

strangers, grazing in your semantic fields.

New Year 2005
When David came back from the nursing home that first time I was
in a panic; resentful, bitter, feeling trapped – everything. I had

continued to keep a notebook from time to time and, looking back at the entries made then, I could see that I had two priorities; the first was to look after David and care for him at home without going completely off my head, and the second was to keep my own work going.

The first involved accessing services and I was about to learn a great deal about that. My work was important because I could see that if eventually it were to come to nursing home care, and having learnt its terrifying cost, I would have to be financially self-sufficient. Apart from that, work kept me sane.

To my surprise there was a lot more help after the false start of the failed nursing home and it was probably the drastic step of David going there and then being rejected from it that made people sit up and take notice of our needs. First there was the care manager. She helped with the daunting form-filling which enabled us to secure finance for care services at home, which was what made the real difference between coping and not coping. The front line of action were the district nurses who called every week and prepared David's syringes. There was a rota of carers who came in daily, enabling me to get out to work. Then we had visits from the "older person's psychiatrist". He may have been a specialist for older people but he seemed quite young himself with a wide range of interests in all things cultural which suited David just fine. He spent a long time getting to know David, his past career with the Organisation and his poetry, and proposed getting him on some memory enhancing drugs in the near future. The doctor too began to take David's state of mind seriously, and to keep a reassuring eye on how I was coping as well. Then there was the "Admiral nurse". Admiral nurses are specialist nurses whose role is to provide practical and emotional support for carers and families of people with dementia and I was lucky enough to have one in my area. She was perhaps the most understanding person I had come across and provided opportunity and space to let off steam and to indulge without blame in self-pity, guilt, grief and all the many emotions that had been building up. Last but not the least in this package of provision, every two months there was the opportunity for David to go into respite allowing me to take a week off, whether quietly at home or taking a break away. The respite was specifically for people with conditions like David's and much more suitable for him than the nursing home that he had tried with such disastrous results. I found myself on a more even course than I had been six months before, with more time and space for my own thoughts and more able to cope. I realised that I had been so wrapped up in the routine of David and the carers that I was losing sight of the person that David used to be and the relationship that we used to have. Now I could allow myself to remember.

The Christmas period passed off peacefully and two weeks into the new year I needed to make a trip to London. There would be time for a morning's shopping, before a meeting in the afternoon in connection with a project that I had been bidding for. It was great to put on a business outfit and join the morning commuters. Leaving the station, I boarded a bus to Oxford Street. Not far from Selfridges was the building where, back in the seventies, I had gone for my own interviews with the Organisation, which led to the posting to Tehran and to meeting David. A cheerful, unstuffy atmosphere had reigned in that office which was in the heart of the mini-skirted, flared-trousered, long-haired, psychedelic, poster-buying shopping area, just off Oxford Street. Nearest tube station, Bond Street. This was where the foreign students liked to come. This had been David's part of town.

I got off the bus, wondering if I could identify the building after so long. It had been sold some years ago – probably redeveloped and unrecognizable, I thought, as I walked along. Then I paused as recognition clicked into place. Yes, that was it; the steps were the same, although the nameplates and logos on the entrance were all quite different. I remembered how it had been on the half-dozen occasions I had visited in the days before David and I met. Maybe, on some of those visits, I had passed him in the corridors without knowing. I tried to imagine life for him then, at the time when his career with the Organisation was taking off.

The regional directorates had been on the third floor; Europe, South America, Asia. Middle East and North Africa directorate, MENA, was where David had worked for two of the three years since his return from Nigeria, the first having been spent acquiring more academic skills doing a Master's degree in linguistics. These last two years had been hectic, due not just to the pace of work but because the rest of his life was in turmoil too. Controller MENA had been helpful in this respect and two months off work the previous summer had given David space to get himself together. The hospital stay of 1972 was behind him and he had no intention of re-visiting either the actual place or the memory of it. He felt new and refreshed. Now he had a project – "*a honey of a project*", he called it to himself – and he was putting a lot into it. It was "*the Saudi Project*".

Since the oil crisis of seventy-three, Saudi Arabia had been pumping oil and banking dollars at an astounding speed. Petro-dollars were piling up trouble for many poor countries, but in Saudi itself the Organisation was pleased to suggest ideas for spending some of the revenue beneficially. For David it was like *carte blanche* to put into practice theories of language-teaching acquired in his recent academic year. ESP – English for Special Purposes –was the new currency and the King Abdul Aziz University, Saudi Arabia English project was going to be David's opportunity to show what could be done. Already he was looking forward to writing it up into an academic paper once the project was under way.

David's office on the third floor was wood and glass-panelled, for this was the era before open-plan completely took over office space, so David could see and be seen while still enjoying his private work-space. On the desk a pile of academic tomes occupied one side, in-tray and out-tray sat on top of each other, drafts of letters, office memos and messages to be telexed were arranged on a table awaiting attention. It was still the age of typewriters and secretaries: one secretary took care of the work of three colleagues, one of whom put his head round the door now.

"Martin!" David exclaimed. "Just the chap! I need you! Which of these sites is the one for us in Jeddah?"

"David, what's all this about?"

David indicated the stack of papers, "University Language Centre. Servicing the medical school, agricultural college and the rest of the university." And before his friend could get a word in he continued in rapid flow. "Language of instruction? English of course! Importance of language centre? Top priority! Money no object. Brief to yours truly? Find site, equip as per state of the art, develop courses – ESP expertise essential – recruit and train staff, all to be up and running nine months from now. State opening scheduled, by His Highness... etc. etc."

"You're a lucky chap! Did you know that?" The colleague smiled indulgently. "So what advice can I help with?"

David pointed to some plans spread out on his desk. "These are the locations we've been offered for the Centre." David laid out three sets of plans on the desk in front of them. "None of them is actually what you would go for, given the choice, but they're in a hurry. The time scale is too short to commission a new-build so we have to make the best of it. Now, what we have here is ..." – he paused, unfolding more papers, rearranging and smoothing them out – "... number one, a complex of warehouse buildings, much work needed to convert and improve; number two, the former boys' high school – it's become redundant since a new building was opened last year; and number three, believe it or not, a disused lemonade factory. This one is also redundant because the company has moved to a new site out of town."

His colleague looked at the drawings with interest. "Where are they in relation to the campus?"

"All three of them are near enough to the main university complex to be viable," David replied. "What do you think?"

"The boys' school would seem the obvious choice. At least it would have the right sort of rooms for teaching in, air-conditioning presumably? Staff room? That kind of thing?"

"That's exactly what I would have thought, but they seem less than keen on it. Anyway, I'm flying out on Monday to have a look, and to look at staff accommodation as well, which is pretty crucial."

The colleague nodded agreement.

"We're working on staff contracts at the moment and living conditions will be important. Recruitment starts next month with ads in the Times Educational Supplement in good time."

"You've got plenty to do. Have you got time for a beer at lunch time?"

"Of course! Then some shopping. A light-weight suit for Saudi and a pair of sunglasses."

The secretary put her head in the door. "Sorry, David. Travel Section just called. Can you ring them about your visa for Saudi?"

"Thanks! Oh and will you take these and get the telexes off?" He handed her the pile of letters and memos, looking at his watch and calculating the hours. "Before two o'clock if you can? Thanks."

As I was to learn subsequently, for the next nine months David had organized a whirlwind of activity, pulling in contributions from all different departments of the Organisation and support from the Foreign Office. He had worked with the Education Recruitment department, drafting advertisements which conveyed his own sense of excitement about the posts, ensuring that the right package of financial and family incentives was in place and alerting university departments in the U.K. so that their brightest M.A. students applied for the posts. He had sat on the panel of interviewers and more or less handpicked the teaching staff he wanted.

The site they settled on in the end was the disused lemonade factory: the idea of turning a lemonade factory into a language centre struck them as amusing but despite the jokes it turned out to be the most suitable and most adaptable. A British firm was appointed for the refurbishment and further visits were needed from David to make sure it was converted to specification. Finally there was the question of appointing the centre director. David was asked to take the job but declined. Having set it up he wanted to move in a wider field. A specialist academic with plenty of practical experience was appointed.

Those months, I reflected, must have been the ideal antidote to David's personal problems. His Saudi project would have allowed him to put the nightmare of those white corridors behind and could have left little time for artistic activities on the psychedelic side. David went on to create what became the model and byword for self-financing education projects overseas and the Organisation set up a new department, Overseas Education Projects, to commission more revenue-earning projects, which could be used to fund its other, non-commercial cultural events.

David spent another year in MENA. It was the same year in which I joined the Organisation but I was packed straight off to Teheran without even a stint in the London office, so at that point our paths didn't cross. At the end of that year David himself was head-hunted to Teheran to lead the Organisation's educational activity in what was now becoming its largest overseas directorate.

The Shah of Iran had just celebrated the 2000th anniversary of his Pahlavi dynasty, with peacock pomp and flourish, in the ruins of Persepolis. His Imperial Majesty's face was firmly turned towards the West and the Organisation was keen to take advantage. David relished the challenge.

So we met in Teheran and it felt very auspicious. I remembered the occasion clearly, in the cellar bar of the Xanadu restaurant, on a quiet *kuche*, or side street, off the main thoroughfares of the city, on a Saturday night, along with friends and colleagues from the office. This place was favoured by expatriates like us, especially the French from the *Alliance Française* and Germans from the *Goethe-Institut*, and our group was surrounded by smoke and the noise of conversation in several different languages.

Our second encounter would be at the Organisation's office, at Monday morning "prayers". This was the regular office briefing session, which took place in the Director's suite and in which all the London-based staff took part. David's reputation had gone before him. His arrival had been looked forward to by the language-centre staff and a process of intellectual ferment began to bubble and seethe. Expansions were planned, new language centres and projects opened around the country, new contracts were signed with businesses and government organizations, a publishing project, a video-making project, a professional teachers' association, new teacher-training courses, and the list went on. Weekends were filled with trips to the mountains and gatherings of friends and colleagues at one or other of the favourite restaurants. In summertime a popular venue was Leon's, an open-air Russian restaurant which offered *blinis* with caviar fresh from the Caspian Sea, washed down with vodka from bottles encased in several inches of ice.

Those had been heady times, I thought, as I headed back to Charing Cross and the train home after a successful meeting and some satisfactory shopping. I was back by six o'clock – later than I had intended but still in reasonable time to transform my role.

But here David and the carer had had a bad day. David had been "seeing" people and things which were not there. I had tried to explain to the carer about the spooks, their underlying causes and how to deal with them but the carer simply felt David was drinking too much. I try to tell her that I don't think he does because most of what he pours himself is left in the glass and just gets thrown away; in any case he's very determined and – with his sense of time shot to pieces – there is no point in telling him that he should wait till 5 o'clock to have a whisky. He had fallen and splashed wine on the sitting room carpet and been thoroughly restless throughout the day – a wet and grey day – and had now retired to the bathroom. The carer was not sure if he was in trouble there or just annoyed with her for trying to control him. Anyway I told her to get off home as she has a long way to travel and a train to catch, and that I would look after him.

After she has gone I go to find David in the bathroom. I quickly realise that the cause of the day's confusion and restlessness and the unwanted spooky visitors has probably been constipation as he was there, sitting on the loo, unable to move, trousers down and shoes mixed up in the trouser-ends – completely stuck.

It's been an eye-opener and it has taken me some time to realise just what this particular problem can do to the mental faculties, especially of someone so impaired as David now is. It can bring on confusion, hallucinations, loss of speech functions and God knows what else. When I get to him, David has lost all mobility and is unable to get off the loo unassisted. His speech has gone and he can barely nod his head, with moist and sunken jaw, in response to my queries. My ability to empathise means, however, that I still imagine he is conscious of the dreadful indignity of the situation. The WC and surrounds were a brown and smelly mess, somewhat like a farmyard in winter, although I have seen cleaner and smelled fresher farmyards.

So role transformation involves dealing with this. First get him off the loo, onto the wheelchair and into the bedroom: next, back in the bathroom, clean up the mess from the seat, "flush and brush" with liberal amounts of bleach: next get him back from bedroom to bathroom to get cleaned up and changed into clean pyjama trousers. By now he is so exhausted that he just wants to go to bed.

I leave him peacefully in bed – at least I think and hope so. Making a meal for myself is pure relaxation after this. A day of contrasts, you might say.

I went in to David later, before going to bed myself. I wanted to tell him my news, that my bid for the project had been accepted. His face lit up! He can still relate to words like "bid" and "tender" and "proposal accepted" and, above all to "project", one of his favourite ideas. I had made some hot chocolate and proposed a cheery toast, "to projects!" A moment like old times despite the role reversal!

THE HOWL COMING OUT OF ASIA

The Emperor
Now the steppenwolf is on the prowl
Listen   The howl coming out of Asia
I live my life my back to mirrors
I dream of the crystal open town
I dream that peace is with us
and I am able to face her
able to enter and drown   drown

Now the glass is looking at me
Expects an answer   an image
It does not like my twisted face
I assume the rags of majesty
step into the toils of grace
it will be a long long voyage
in the glass a misty winter tree

See the waves stammer as the wind
flings in the clouds and birds
of spring   I put out leaves
The river at my roots shines
There are nests songs wives
I feel the earth wheel as the herds
approach   My people eat light rains[1]

Teheran, December 1979
We had been married for more than a year and social and working
life revolved around the Organisation in Teheran. Despite the
political storm clouds, everything was buzzing: work was exciting,
and in our spare time there were historical sites to visit and
weekend walks in the mountains. Our first springtime together we
walked the hillside paths which led to villages on terraced hillsides.
A favourite route was to leave the car at the roadside and follow
tracks which were the sole access to two mountain villages. The
tracks led up through a steep-sided valley, sometimes hugging the
mountainside and sometimes taking us along the side of a stream.

Sometimes we had to flatten ourselves against the rock wall as boys leading heavily-laden mules and donkeys made their way at a brisk pace down the steep path through mud and half-melted snow. They scarcely glanced at us, despite our incongruous western clothes and cameras. We photographed the mountains, the icy streams where the winter snows rushed down the valleys, and the walnut and almond trees in blossom. And more than anything we photographed each other. Another trip was little more than an hour's drive from the city to a popular ski resort. We skied in jeans and jumpers and anything that was warm and the sunshine was so brilliant it left us dazed for the rest of the week! And on the drive back to the city in the evening we could stop at a roadside chai-khane, a tea house where we sat on carpets and drank bitter tea, flavoured with dried limes and chunks of clear sugar and ate white cheese and flat-bread with sliced red onions. Usually a hubble-bubble was passed around at which David would take a turn. The atmosphere was warm and welcoming although I sensed that as a woman, usually the only one there, I had to make myself unobtrusive. Away from the ski slopes this was a men's world.

In the last days of rule of the Shah – self-styled "*His Imperial Majesty Shahanshah, King of Kings, head of the Pahlavi dynasty, ruler from the Peacock Throne*" – as the revolutionary movement gathered pace, expatriates lived a strange life. Some days we went to work, other days the message came that the streets were unsafe and we should stay at home. Embassies were beginning to repatriate their staff's dependants and there was a feeling at work of things winding down. Christmas was a time for receiving refugees, the teachers who had been called back to the hub from the Organisation's six language centres around the country. David and I gave hospitality to several of them at our apartment. We lived in the Armenian quarter of the city, an area of apartments and little local shops where we could still buy wine and spirits. Parties and a sense of danger mingled. But the apprehension of the Armenian citizens was becoming apparent and the buying of alcohol, although not yet banned, took on a different, almost illicit meaning.

From the windows of our fourth floor apartment just south of Tahkte-e-Jamshid, we looked down the length of the city to where the bazaar district in the south was a blur in the distance. It was from there, however, that events were being shaped and not from the northern summit where the Palace – and all those in it or visiting it – were, according to what we had heard, in disarray.

David had been in Isfahan three weeks earlier, representing the Organisation at a conference at the university. Among the academics the word was that those in power – and those advising them – knew nothing of what was brewing.

"They just have not grasped it," one told David. "What's going on is a big, big thing. It's not just a series of riots, not protests like those you saw last year: this is coming from the people: it's bubbling up from below. This is an insurrection."

That word produced a frisson. Back in the capital David passed on what he had been told to the embassy, who nodded their heads with interest and promised to note it and pass it on in due course.

Meanwhile the insurrection gathered pace. Marches were more frequent, women who had never done so before adopted the all-enveloping *chador*.

"You should get yourself a *chador*," David told me one morning as we prepared to set out for the office.

And I had replied equally firmly, "That's something I'm just not prepared to do! You won't catch me hiding myself under a disguise from the Middle Ages!"

"Buy one. Keep it in your handbag. You could find it useful some time…"

I shook my head. "The whole point of what is going on here is to free things up, to liberalise."

David didn't insist. It was not his style to lay down the law or to act the heavy-handed husband.

In the mosques at Friday prayers a thousand duplicates of small cassettes flown in from France played and replayed the words of the cleric who dared to oppose the King of Kings and break the vaunted bonds-of-iron which bound his people to him.

Among the students at the language centre the mood was excited: censorship of the press had been relaxed though not abolished; plans were being made and dreams dreamed for the new liberal society. Nevertheless, on the streets the *mujahideen* were out and making their presence felt. Excitement and danger were in the air in equal parts. In the uncertainty, classes were closed and staff-members were repatriated. For those who had been there a long time, it was a sad departure.

On one particular morning there was a leaving party – if party was the right word: more of a wake, perhaps. I had volunteered to bring the drinks and had encountered the largest demonstration so far, converging on the main Ferdowsi Avenue. There was no hope of getting there by car but it seemed of vital importance to get through with the two bags of drinks! I had decided to take a route through the *kuches*, the side-streets, to the Centre and, finding a space, I parked the car and locked it. At this point I did somewhat regret the lack of a *chador* which can conceal any amount of awkward luggage. In spite of the bitter East wind I took off my coat and draped it over the two carrier bags with their clinking cargo then dodged round a few back streets and negotiated the remaining two hundred yards of the wide Ferdowsi Avenue, where the demonstration was vast and noisy.

"*Mard bar Shah! Mard bar Amerika!*" The rhythmic chant threatening death to the Shah and to America was intimidating, but I scuttled though and made a dash for the Centre's compound. The tall blue gates were shut but the *farash* on duty let me in through the small inset door, greeting me with an uneasy smile.

This leaving party was a subdued occasion. The director of the language centre made presentations to the teachers who were leaving and wished them all good luck. In the background we could hear clearly the chants of the crowd marching in the streets outside. Towards the end I found myself seated next to our ambassador. I wondered why he should be gracing such a relatively humble event as a teachers' leaving party. He looked tired and as if he was just glad to have somewhere to sit down away from the pressure of events. He told me about his recent interview with the Shah and how he had told the Shah he should at least feel proud of his people for showing such determination and persistence. I didn't think His Imperial Majesty could have found this very consoling but I was flattered to feel I was hearing history from the inside.

For David it was a disappointing time from a professional and career point of view. Having been head-hunted for the post, he had worked hard to make a success of it; projects were getting under way and his enthusiasm had fired his team: but now everything was winding down. We hoped that wouldn't be for long and that things would soon get busy again.

With the office closed, it was an unusually peaceful time at home in the apartment, up there above the city. Down below the marches continued and at night time, increasingly, firing could be heard. Teheran in winter has a quality of light and air, between grey and white; the bare trees, the distant mountains to the North, the dryness of the air, all contributed to a sense of brittleness. Each morning when I went outside, putting the key to the car door, unfailingly I leapt and cursed as the static from the car door hit me.

We mostly stayed indoors however and read books, listened to Pink Floyd and tuned in to the BBC's World Service. For extra company there was the cat; it scrabbled up the outside of the building, from ground floor window-sill, to second floor projecting ledge, thence to the third floor's air-conditioning unit and the final, heart-stopping effort, a frantic scrabble up the sheer wall where the only claw-hold was the rough-cast exterior plaster which coated the building. Puss-cat always made it safely, to enjoy milk and food outside on the kitchen balcony and then we allowed it to come inside for company before making the perilous descent. One evening I ran the tape-recorder and recorded the firing going on outside in the city punctuated by the mewing of the cat, indoors with us for its evening visit. I kept that tape for years and wondered what had become of the cat when we left; I hope it was a survivor.

For the two of us it was a time of hiatus, of holding our breath, in the cold, cold winter air, as the country also held its breath and waited for the outcome. David occupied his hours of enforced leisure with diagrams of the universe of language. With A3 sheets of graph-paper, pencils, eraser and differently-coloured pens, he highlighted the dimensions and structured pairs and quartets of abstractions, mapping speech-acts and patterns of interactivity into taut and symmetrical designs: "Logic," "Style" and "Force," opposed "Attention," "Author" and "Scope". "Point of View," "Framing" and "Agenda" stood face to face with "Register," "Code" and "Dialect". The four compass points were connected on three levels by abstractions like "Field," "Circuit" and "Tenor" on the one hand, "Experiential Grammar" and ... I couldn't read the rest and gave up as abstractions heaped upon abstractions, but happy that David was enjoying the mental exercise and had roped in a colleague, on similarly enforced absence from the office but living near enough to get over to the apartment and join in the feast of concepts. I felt for the colleague's wife who had small children to care for and was not often able to come over and I assumed that, with a young family, mother and children would soon be on their way home as families were being urged to leave, and the pressure was greatest on those with children. A week later they had gone, but so too had the Shah.

"*Shah raft! Shah raft!*" The maid repeated over and over, the day after the incredible event, "The Shah has gone, the Shah has gone!"

"Khomeini will come back now," I said, "And you will hate all of us westerners".

"*Nemisheh, nemisheh!*" Fatimeh had replied. "We won't hate you." And she explained to me that all people who were "of the Book" had no need to fear. I was unsure if it would hold good for the Jewish traders who were selling off their stock of carpets as quickly as they could in preparation for leaving the country, or for Americans who were threatened with death by placards and demonstrations on every street corner, but Fatimeh's goodwill towards David and me was not in doubt. Fatimeh had been David's maid before David and I had joined forces. She was a small bird-like lady, with a leathery face, pinched cheeks and a forceful manner of speaking. My attempts at Farsi and the difficulty I had in understanding Fatimeh appeared to exasperate her and she resorted to extravagant gestures to clarify her meaning. When she finished work in the afternoons she would throw her *chador* around herself with a sweeping motion and then make herself small under it and disappear into the anonymity of the streets. Fatimeh approved of our marriage, but made it clear that David had been her employer before I had come along. She always ironed David's shirts before touching my clothes. My maid was called Pari and was quite different both in appearance and character from Fatimeh. Where Fatimeh was small and wiry Pari was plump and roundly built. Where Fatimeh was forceful and didactic, Pari was accommodating and easy-going. I didn't want to put Pari out of a job when we came back from leave in England as a married couple, and so, for a while, we had two maids. Needless to say, it didn't work; the two women did not get on at all well. In the end Pari left, saying she had found another job. It was just as well, as the apartment was not big enough for two people to clean it.

Soon after Christmas the refugee teachers were sent on their way, their contracts terminated early and travel arrangements facilitated back to London, there to look for new jobs, teaching their so-saleable language in different parts of the world. Over the next few weeks the pressure for other staff to leave became stronger. It surprised me to find that the act of marrying had made me a "dependent" in the eyes of officialdom. Many wives resisted the call to leave, sticking by their men. I was beginning to feel slightly queasy about it all; not just the threat of violence in the air – something else seemed to be changing. I was losing the taste for gin-and-tonic for one thing, and, while it was really too early to say anything, I knew what that might signify, and thought perhaps it might be wise to join the leavers. Then the airport was closed, so the question was irrelevant. But when diplomacy opened the airport for three days to take wives and families away, I was one of them. The phone call came after dark one evening as we sat together, making plans. David stroked my hair. "Well, my pretty one, it looks as if you will have to go."

I sighed.

"And leave your poor lover here all on his own!"

This was difficult. "You'll be back home in a week or so, they can't keep you on here for long," I told him. "It's not safe. And there's nothing to do."

Rather than bewail the separation, our thoughts turned to what would happen when David would be back as well and where we would be sent next.

"The Organisation is going to have so many spare staff on its hands they won't know what to do with us straight away."

"So let's make some plans ready to put to them!" And we dreamed a dream of a year back in the UK together which I hoped – secretly, because it was still just such a faint suspicion on my part that I hadn't dropped any hint to David – would include the start of our family.

"Do you think they might offer you a study year?" I suggested. It was not unknown for this to be agreed, where it could be seen to benefit the Organization as well as the person concerned.

"It's an exciting thought," David agreed. "I could do an M.Phil. in a year and I have no lack of ideas for it."

"Followed by a new posting a year on from that, when the backlog has been sorted out...?"

Thus we laid our plans, hoping that the Organisation might see things the same way.

"Better be careful though, don't bank on it!" David cautioned. "Remember what John Lennon says: '*Life is what happens when you are busy making other plans!*'"

"OK," I agreed. "But there's no harm in having the plan up our sleeves!"

Later on experience was to prove how true that saying was but there was no shadow of that at present. Here in Teheran, normal life was at a standstill. The airport was closed after the Shah's departure and Khomeini's return, until, for a space of three days, it was re-opened for families and dependents to fly out.

Coaches had been hired and the British contingent was ordered to report at the embassy summer compound, well away from the city centre, in two days time. It was a sombre departure on a grey and chilly winter morning.

We flew out on a VC10 of the RAF and, as the pilot announced that the plane was leaving Iranian airspace some of the passengers gave a cheer. I didn't join in or share that sentiment. My own feeling was regret that the three years which had been so exciting and full of significant events were ending in this inconclusive way, even though it was exciting to be going back to England. A pregnancy test was top of my to-do list and I definitely expected that David would be out in three or four weeks, but it was sad all the same.

In Cyprus we were checked again and a woman Army officer took my details:

"Name of the head of your family?"

"Ah," I hesitated. "My husband and I...we tend to share that position."

The officer was unimpressed and wrote down David's name.

The last leg of flight was to Gatwick Airport, where my parents were waiting with the car in the snowy February landscape.

David did not leave in the next few weeks. In fact it was three months before he arrived back at Heathrow airport with most of our belongings in a very large tin trunk.

In the meantime there were three months of being a daughter once again. How strange to be back in ones own teen-age bedroom and to find the familiar rose-patterned wall-paper still on the walls. My husband and our old exotic life were a million miles away, discounted almost as if they had never existed.

My pregnancy was confirmed soon after and I told David on a crackly phone line. He was clearly moved and excited. My parents too – a first and longed-for grandchild. Three months passed slowly. Phone lines to Iran were erratic, so we did not have too many conversations. But David wrote letters with hair-raising stories of journeys round the provinces, closing down the Organisation's centres. One of his tasks was to auction off several loads of equipment, whilst adhering to strict civil service rules. He described the procedure. "Bids for items have to be made in brown, sealed envelopes but, if you can imagine masked and armed *mujahideen* telling me how much and not a penny more they were prepared to pay for tape-players, desks and whiteboards complete with board-markers, I couldn't exactly insist on the strict letter of the law!"

Being a daughter for this length of time proved hard work and it was May before I went to pick David up at the airport. As I waited at the arrivals gate all the passengers off his flight appeared to have passed through and I was quite in despair. When eventually he appeared, tall, curly-haired, tired, but smiling through those round glasses, I clung to him with tears flowing freely.

"Hey! Pretty One" – the familiar pet name made the tears flow faster – "What's up?" He asked.

"I thought you weren't coming! Why were you so long?"

He pointed to the pile of luggage and the enormous tin trunk.

"That's what held me up. It's got our life inside!"

What next? A year in England; a year of post-graduate studies for David, the small house of our dreams in a university town, and the birth of our first son, Joe, in the autumn. Then a posting in Europe and the birth of our second son, Nigel. We were busy and happy, and after four years, another new posting saw David as the organization's director in a small but friendly Gulf State. It was a lovely life and we probably didn't realize how lucky we were. Until the signs began: as yet unclear what tale the signs were telling.

THE COMING SHOCK

The Tower

Those who stay inside the tower
bluffing out the dragon's breath
forget the sun's a blaze of souls.
They revolve inside the hour
stasis stasis in their bowels
in their skulls the spoon of death
lobotomising dreams of power

Those who on the turrets stand
gazing on the dragon's scales
noting liquid plays of light
will not fall upon the land
when the bolting thunder strikes.
They will hoist their leprous sails
and drown where drowning's planned.

Those whose towers are the locked
molecules of frozen light
where the stone is latticework
see the coming lightning shock
watch the dragons in the murk
fetch the starchild from the night
write the last word in their book.

Muscat, April 1986

David handed me a gin and tonic, clinking with ice and slices of limes and remarked happily, "Life is really rather pleasant!"

The air was hot and humid but still bearable enough to sit outside for evening drinks. The evening call to prayer from the mosque a quarter of a mile away punctuated the insistent hum of air-conditioners from the house. Time to relax.

"Life is really rather pleasant," he repeated.

I smiled. It was David's regular refrain at the end of a working day, when there was no official reception or meal to attend, and we sat outside on the patio with the light fading and the stars pricking through the velvet darkness. The phrase aptly summed up David's enjoyment of all that we had: his job, his work, the contacts it gave him and the satisfaction at the end of a day, a family provided for and ideal surroundings. And it was beautiful here, especially at this time of day, as darkness fell. Off to our right, the line of the sea was punctuated by distant specks – the lights of oil tankers at anchor, waiting their turn to continue up the Gulf towards the Straits of Hormuz, to the oil depots of Iran and the Gulf States. The night-time air was as warm as during the day and darkness brought no relief because the mountains behind, devoid of vegetation in any shape or form, were night-storage heaters of solid rock, casting the heat of the day back until the early hours of the morning. Up until about April it was pleasant, the air velvety and caressing, as we sat out on the stone terrace flanked on three sides by the house.

Two small boys were riding a bicycle and tricycle respectively in loops and circles until called away to bed. The older one, Joe, born in England, some nine months after the revolution in Iran, had spent the first year of his life in an English village. I hoped he might go to the village school, but a new posting in Europe denied that possibility. At present he was performing stylish circles on a red bicycle, from which the trainer wheels had recently been removed. Nigel, the younger one, born two years later, was pedalling furiously in circles, his knees almost touching his nose with each push on the pedals of his sturdy yellow tricycle.

I am aware that I have telescoped the years. After the unexpected exit from Iran there was a year in England and the birth of our first son. That was followed by the European posting, which I have mentioned, to Germany, where cultural activities were a priority and David brought poets and writers to give readings from their works. He worked closely, too, with academics in linguistics, initiated exchanges with teacher training colleges between the two countries and collaborated on programmes of an educational and cultural nature for a television network. Nigel, our second son was born there and for me the time passed in a blend of domesticity, some textbook writing, which was a useful form of employment fitting well with the domestic life, and enjoyment of the cultural events which David was organising. Now, four years on, found us posted once again to the Middle East.

Once there had been trading between the Northern and Southern shores of the Persian Gulf; now, following the revolution in Iran and the ensuing war with its neighbour Iraq, trade was reduced to a trickle, barely more than the smuggling of cigarettes from one side to the other. Now there was the tanker war with the bombing of oil carriers, as they queued to pass through the straights at the top end of the Gulf, which made smuggling even more dangerous.

Oman was then – and still is – a pearl on the Gulf coast, not far on the map from Iran, where we had first met, but different in so many respects. This friendliest of Gulf states where we now lived, although it scrutinised and controlled our entry rigorously, held a hospitable and tolerant attitude towards foreigners, Its rulers expected us to stick to a dress code which would not offend their religious beliefs, but accepted invitations to our receptions and allowed us to enjoy our life-style without comment. Hence the cheerful clinking of gin and tonics as David and I relaxed on the terrace at the end of the day.

The last of the light had almost gone and the noise of traffic on the main road had stopped. The darkness was humid and its warmth was tangible, reflected off the rocks, the sand and the roads around us. Cricket calls added texture to the darkness; the moon rose over the shoulder of the house and the cry from the mosque was a reminder of the hour.

The following day we were due to fly up to the northern outpost of the country, the point where the straits narrowed and where only twenty miles separated the northern shores of the Gulf from the southernmost coast of Iran. David had to visit an educational project there, a new vocational training college, which the Organisation was backing with funds and support. I didn't usually go along on these working trips but this was somewhere unusual and interesting. It was all very well to be the supportive wife at cultural events and the hostess when it fell to us to entertain; I enjoyed it immensely and met interesting people, but the chance to go somewhere quite off the beaten track and unfrequented was not to be missed.

As I went indoors to make our meal I had to agree that, yes, life really was rather pleasant.

A stiff early morning breeze was blowing the following day as we flew north up the line of the coast. We were two of eight passengers taking advantage today of the regular Twin-Otter service from the capital up to the tiny airport at the tip of the northern peninsular. The children were still asleep when we left home at 6am in the Organisation's Range Rover with the office driver at the wheel. After dropping us off at the airport he would do the school run for me before reporting back to the office for duty.

Now the little aircraft droned along, rocked slightly from side to side by the wind. The coastline was straight and we could pick out familiar landmarks easily. Inland to the left the line of the Jebel, the mountain range, and the forts we knew from weekend trips, Nakhl, Rustaq, El Hazm. To the right, on the edge of the sea, the small towns of Seeb, Barka and the village of Sumail with its tiny islet and curving, shining, shell-lined bay. There was one stop en route, at Sohar where, as we came in to land, the strength of the wind was whipping the branches of palm trees to a frenzy and I held on to my seat and my breath, as we swayed and rocked from side to side. Then we were down with a bump and the pilot entirely relaxed, which was reassuring. When the door was opened, salt, hot air and grit blew in from the runway. A few passengers departed and new ones came on board, two gentlemen wearing *dish-dashas* and a woman in dazzling pink wrapping her black *abbaya* tightly around her as the wind tugged at it.

Ten minutes later we were up again, air-borne above the tops of the flapping palm trees. Now to our right several oil tankers could be seen steaming up the coast and further still, a group of them, bunched together, riding at anchor. This was the queue for the passage through the narrow straights.

As we neared the furthest tip of the peninsula, the mountain range came crowding down towards the shoreline until, finally, mountains were all that could be seen, rising precipitously out of the sea, jagged cliffs, the colour of cardboard, and the sea like deep amethyst, flecked with white and breaking on the rocks.

We were approaching our destination now, although where, in this array of crags and cliffs, space might be found to put a plane down, was a mystery to me. My mind was taken off that question though. For, as we circled and climbed high over a rocky peak, gaining height, I could see like a geography lesson the extent of the narrow straits laid out below. Beyond the straits, just twenty miles wide, the northern coast – it must be Iran – was quite visible. But between there and where we circled were two smoking hulls, two plumes of rising smoke, two oil tankers. I drew my breath in. Here indeed was the tanker war, usually remote, read about in newspapers and reported on World Service radio. In 1986 few people had satellite television and local television hardly referred to it. But this sign of the current conflict of the late twentieth century was a mere matter of feet below us, just for a few minutes, and then was lost from view.

The plane circled around. Jagged cliffs and dangerous rocks were all I could see, but the pilot knew better. Bringing the plane over one more peak and then flying out to sea, he circled around and set the plane on a course low over the harbour and landed us neatly and without fuss on the airstrip in the little township, set in the bay between two arms of mountains.

Now that we were down, that brief glimpse of warfare, seen from above, was like an unreal memory. Down here was a sheltered enclosed world, whose limited access and isolated nature, despite the searing heat, had more the peaceful feel of a Scottish island settlement. While David went off to his meetings for the rest of the day I relaxed by the pool of the small guest-house. Next morning there was to be a ceremony, a presentation of books from their office to the new college. I would be there to swell the numbers and add to the Organisation's presence.

It was David's custom to rise at six and go running, taking advantage of the relative cool of the early morning. From home he usually took the car and parked near the beach which stretched for several kilometres of hard, flat sand. It was an ideal place for running and attracted several like-minded souls. As well as keeping him fit David found the rush of oxygen to the brain set him up for the day. To miss running was a real deprivation and the day would begin badly.

Here on the peninsula, where the entire coast was made of rock, and space to run was limited, he decided to do circuits of the township's community sports ground. I was aware when he left and turned over for another spell of sleep.

But David was back early, limping into the room and massaging his left foot. I came awake to ask what was up.

"Cramp," David replied. "Ouch! It keeps coming back!"

"Try stretching your foot back – here, let me help. Like this." I stretched his leg out straight bending the toes back towards the shin. "Any better?"

"Yeah, it's improving. I had to stop half way through. Bloody annoying. I only managed ten minutes."

I was sympathetic, knowing how he relied on his run to give him his morning high.

"Never mind. Have a shower. Or have a swim, now the cramp's gone. The pool looks nice. I'm going to swim!"

"Hmm, I might." He was subdued.

The book presentation went well. The *Wali*, the local governor, wore ceremonial robes over the usual white dish-dash and his *khanjar* gleamed in its silver scabbard. The librarian displayed his collection of books and was pleased with the new acquisitions. And the students, neat in white robes and embroidered caps, practiced their English on us.

Since the return flight was not till the evening, at my request we had been offered a trip on the *Wali*'s ship, a wooden dhow with a powerful engine. The dhow was taking passengers and supplies to the most remote and isolated fishing villages of the peninsula and this rare opportunity was too good to miss. To my mind the coastline bore a close resemblance to Scandinavian fjords, and the tall cliffs which, from the air, had appeared the colour of dark sandstone, from sea level were a forbidding grey.

The captain took the ship out of the harbour and headed along the coast for some kilometres before turning her sharply landwards towards a barely perceptible gap in the cliffs that opened up as we approached. It revealed a long narrow inlet where the sea was a flat calm and along which we chugged for what seemed like several kilometres more. Looking back I got the impression of being in a completely landlocked stretch of water, the open sea having long since disappeared from sight. Twenty minutes of this and a small settlement came into view, the village we were heading for, and the first stop. Here fishing families made up the population, dependent on supplies from the township and especially for their fresh water. We could see the tall blue freshwater container set back on the narrow stretch of rocky beach. We had passed a vessel which looked much like a landing craft, with "Peninsular Development Board" stencilled on its side, painted in bright tones of blue and white and carrying huge containers painted in the same shade of blue and similarly stencilled, which would be winched ashore and exchanged for the empty ones.

"So that's how they manage for water. I wonder how they coped before this system was set up?"

We stopped only briefly at the village, just long enough to unload some supplies and a passenger or two and to pick up others. Then off again, back down the jagged fjord, the water a deep blue – deeper than blue – and the foam creaming from the bow. David and I settled on wooden benches in the stern, shaded by a canvas awning, and enjoyed the rest of the trip. There were two more stops and as we sailed into one fjord and then another all sense of direction disappeared. As the sun began to set, several passengers took mats out and performed prayers on the worn wooden deck. And as the sun sank lower, we returned to the harbour. It had been an unforgettable few hours.

The light in the shadow of the mountains was beginning to fade as our small plane took off, but as we gained height, the sun was still above the horizon. We could see the burnt-out oil tankers, although the smoke had died down now. The plane circled and turned to follow the coastline south again.

"How's the foot?" I asked.

"OK, now." But David still looked worried. "It's not the first time, you see. It happened earlier this week. I just didn't mention it."

"Well, it's only a cramp. I can't see that's anything to worry about."

"May be not. But it's a nuisance all the same."

Over the next few months David found himself stopped from running more and more frequently. And that was the beginning of …. well, we didn't know what it was the beginning of. Certainly it was the start of a long and frustrating search to know what was afflicting the left side of David's body.

And by the time we did begin to get an answer – by then – the good times, although we didn't know it, were coming to an end. The bad times were just beginning.

HERE YOU ARE

Only Yours
Here you are yards away
from the wilderness,
a sun spattered
pondside in late May:
extravagant azaleas,
strawberry red rhododendrons,
jonquil yellow flags

Here you are glanced at
by the black and white
tinged with ginger
large omani cat,
trailing a frond of bracken
like a virgin's wedding train.

Here you are chucking
the chin of the baboon
muzzled yellow labrador,
practising sitting
bolt upright
on its hind legs
its spine goldening.

You are
the composition of your smile,
ripe, assured skin
tightening on cheek bones
polished by the sun,
a frazzle of light in your hair
in the lit space that is only yours.

England, May 1994
I look at the photographs which David took in our garden and
which I know he used when writing this poem. They show me
kneeling and caressing a dog and a cat against a dazzle of azaleas

and rhododendrons, a garden pond surrounded by ferns and yellow irises.

At the end of our posting to Muscat we had returned to England and come to live in the old home where I had grown up. It was my dream to live there and carry on the traditions, letting our children experience the freedom of the house and its garden which I had known throughout my childhood. David was growing to love the place too and, because it was within easy commuting distance of London where he would be working, it seemed a good idea all round.

Some notes which I wrote however reveal that all was not well and reflect vividly my worries at that time.

"It may be the onset of the disease. Something is making David retreat into a small social circle and put up barriers against the rest of the world. He doesn't seem to make friends very much outside work. Anyone with a professional interest is an exception – language teaching and linguistics are still his abiding interest, and, of course, anyone within the Organisation, which he regards in any case as extended family. Sometimes I feel cut off from the world around me and trapped inside the head of this person I'm married to, but I just don't understand. David's world seems to be structured along quite different lines from everyone else's; some sort of conceptual schema or metaphysical world. – I really don't know what I am talking about here. – Perhaps his world is entirely made up of symbols and metaphors. Certainly it stands at an angle of several degrees away from the world which most of us know. The songs he makes up and sings with the children are simply surreal. That's deliberate of course. Part of teaching his sons to look differently at the world and to be bold about the absurd. The children love it, but I fear all this could lead them into dangerous regions of unreality."

I write now with hindsight as I look again at the photographs. At the time when they were taken it was impossible to put a finger on anything really wrong.

Soon after our return to England I went with David to see a London specialist about the cramps he was experiencing. We sat side by side in that office as the diagnosis we had feared was confirmed: Parkinson's disease.

Parkinson's. It had an elderly, disabled, wrinkly, worn-out, second-class citizen feel about it. The shock, the blow was intense. Numbness, cold and nausea; as I think of that consulting room, those are the feelings that return. Everything changed – but we were silent: unable to summon appropriate words.

The specialist was cheerful; this was, after all, his field, his everyday work, nothing unusual for him here.

"No need to let this affect your lives!" he told us brightly. "Not to any great extent that is."

It was difficult to think of the right questions to put to him. David tried.

"How fast is it likely to…well, to go on?" David asked.

But again, there was no clear answer to that.

"Can I still do jogging? Play squash?"

Again, the answers were rather vague. "You should keep on doing the exercise that you are used to doing. Don't push yourself, but there's no reason to give it up. Quite the opposite."

We tried to look as if that was helpful.

"But the cramps; they happen more frequently now…" It was a question not a statement.

"The medication should keep them under control," the doctor replied. "Just do as much as you feel like doing."

"And work?"

Here the specialist was only slightly more specific. "If you are thinking of retiring at sixty-five you might perhaps revise that down and think, around sixty."

David was in his very early fifties at that stage.

How is it that in the specialist's consulting room the patient turns into a meek petitioner, grateful simply for crumbs of advice? The advice we got was much too superficial and was handed out probably with the intention not to give us a fright, and to send us away on an upbeat note. But during the meeting I had hardly been able to contain my tears. The specialist obviously thought they were uncalled for.

As we came away I felt stunned – but resolved that we must accept the view that life should go on as usual and Parkinson's must be nothing more than an inconvenience. What is more crucial

– and something that I can only see with hindsight – is that David, from that point on I think, felt entirely undermined.

On the surface our situation looked good. There was still the possibility of another foreign posting and meanwhile I wanted to make the most of this interlude at home. Both boys went to the village school which in itself provided a way of life for mothers, with new friends to meet daily at the school gate. David continued to play a large part in the boys' development; he took them on trips to London at weekends and at half-terms to see films, treating them to meals at Indian or Chinese restaurants. He encouraged them on the computer with painting packages and the latest games. It was the innocent age of Super Mario and Bonecruncher, two of their favourite computer games that I remember.

When the boys moved on to secondary school, David regularly attended parents' evenings, revelling in the glowing reports that were mostly forthcoming for both of them.

But our own social life was different and David was dropping out of any engagements which were remotely sociable. He clearly now found these threatening and hard to handle. I tried to help, and to turn a blind eye to the problems; some might call that "being in denial", but how else could one behave? According to our plans and expectations this should be a time of fulfilment, the years when two small children were growing up with all the excitement and activity that brought with it. But the way that David appeared now to be giving up on himself was alarming, frustrating, and difficult to understand. No-one had told us about depression – least of all the specialist in his West End consulting room – or that depression is something that goes along with Parkinson's. With hindsight I can reproach myself and admit that already this had happened to David. And there were back-pain problems too, really seriously incapacitating him: as I come to write, it is easy to forget about that additional complication.

Four years after our return to England, any thought of a new posting put aside, David decided he would opt for early retirement. From this time on, coping with the changes and trying to keep family life normal and cheerful became considerably more difficult. It had never been easy to read David's mind. His view of the world was so different from most other people's – wasn't this what had attracted me in the first place? – that you could either get caught up inside it or else find yourself completely on the outside.

David bought a book and asked me to read it. It described the life of a man with Parkinson's that I guessed David was seeing himself turning into, wheelchair bound with limbs that jerked and shook uncontrollably. It seemed a very bad book to me and I read a little and put it firmly away. If that was being in denial – well, I certainly was. A Parkinson's Disease Society existed, I was aware, but definitely not for the likes of us. Not for people with two young boys in school and the world before them. Not for people who were busy with life. That book was all about physical symptoms. That there might be more to the disease than physical symptoms was not something that occurred to me, but of course it should have done.

My level of ignorance in this dimension of Parkinson's disease is not unusual. This was not just an unwillingness to face facts but also to face up to the truth that there is more to Parkinson's disease than its physical manifestation. For instance, the strange thing that occurred now was David's inability to finish a task or to meet a deadline, a thing that would have been simply unimaginable just a few years before. There was one particular long piece of writing which he had to complete before his final retirement and it was the most drawn-out process that you could imagine. I discovered that this too is a familiar pattern where Parkinson's is involved: an inability to meet deadlines, even in those who have done exactly that throughout their lives. At the time I found this new phenomenon totally inexplicable.

From then on his withdrawal from social life became more and more apparent and in his last two years with the Organisation, when he was based in London, the demands of handling meetings and chairing discussions became stressful and frightening. These weren't things one could see at the time but only with hindsight. They are the reason why, living at the old family home – the adventure which we had embarked on with high expectations – was, on one level, also a time of confusion and distress, mixed in with the cheerful and busy family life which, on another level, we led.

I can't remember exactly when it became clear that I had to take over the family finances, and also the decision-making on most matters, trying to handle things tactfully and "consult" with David, but in fact making most of the decisions. This was stressful and people, acquaintances, didn't seem to understand at all how it could be so. But why should they?

Close friends and family were different. Robert, our gardener, was one of the most perceptive and solid in being such a reliable and consistent friend and David came to accept him as someone he could be natural with.

A couple of times I took the boys on holiday on our own, once to a Greek island, once back to the Gulf, and once to the West of Ireland to show them the places which I had enjoyed at their age.

After that it became necessary to get to know the ins-and-outs of Social Services procedures; to "access services", as I then learnt to say. Despite the contrast with our previous way of life, it had to be done.

This chapter has telescoped a period of roughly ten years. During that time the boys moved in turn to their secondary school. We acquired the yellow labrador – the one in the photographs, described in the poem – which Joe and Nigel, separately by this time, took on long walks. Cousins came and went for summer holidays. And we, the four of us, took our holiday in France under canvas most years.

David had introduced his sons to the Beatles and our eldest, as I often said, could have gone on "Mastermind" with his inside knowledge of their lives. I returned to University for another year to acquire a qualification that enabled me to find work during the secondary school years.

But all this time the Parkinson's shadow was growing and David – the person I first knew – was increasingly absent. And it was not what we had planned. Life, as has been remarked, is what happens to you when you are busy making other plans. But to become reconciled to this was the most difficult part of it.

Those ten years were a mix of good and bad times, with Parkinson's inexorably exerting its effect along the way. By now we had carers who came and went, some more caring and reliable than others. As some kind of nursing home solution crossed my mind with increasing frequency, I continued to tell myself alternately that we should try a bit longer and then that I had had as much as I could take and everything was becoming a burden. As a distraction I began to write. I worked on a novel which had nothing to do with illness, disability or mental degeneration. At the same time, I kept a diary, where the bottled up frustration and anger and the daily events which caused them could be safely stored. The diary writing was a release but to go further and turn the experiences into something more creative – that would be more satisfying, especially if it could be done in the form of a story.

And that was how "Sarah" was chosen to be the narrator of this story.

"Sarah" is a lot more black and white than her creator and does not suffer from an instinctive tendency to hedge her bets, to justify herself on the one hand and to blame herself on the other, traits which would make for a narrative of tedious introspection. Sarah is someone who can say "This was how it was; this is what happened, this is what I felt – full stop!" Sarah is the person who was needed to tell the story in a way that makes some kind of sense. But she must step back now and allow the writer to take up the threads.

"David" was a different kind of invention. That name, "David", to me (me the writer: not "Sarah"), has always had a gentle, trustworthy, straightforward feel to it, so perhaps the choice of name is that kind of simplification. My own husband, the writer of the poems, was complicated and not at all given to self-revelation; "gentle" was not a word I would have used when I knew him first, although fatherhood certainly brought out that side of his nature. As the illness progressed, his carers and helpers began to refer to him as "warm" and "gentle", which made me wonder if we were talking about the same person. In my head, although not in real life, I held conversations with him where he was still the questing, searching, energetic and dynamic personality I had first known.

So David became the main character in Sarah's more straightforward story. Our sons, whom I did not want to put under the spotlight, made their appearance as Joe and Nigel. Some of our friends were melded into one another, to simplify matters, some episodes and people were simply imagined and time too underwent some stretching and warping. And also now as I continue with the story, Sarah is at my elbow, prompting, ordering me to be clear and I am trying to be truthful in spirit, though truth, like "reality", may well be a different fiction in everyone's head. As I continue, Sarah is letting me keep the names even though you, the reader, now know them to be fictitious.

There was to be a trial period at the nursing home, to see how it worked: the trial ended with a near disaster on the day that David walked out. He did it most likely out of a spirit of independence and a desire to get out and explore on a fine, sunny day, more than with any intention of actually leaving the place behind. Whatever the motivation, he wandered into the park which surrounded the home and got lost, no-one could tell where. The manager called me late in the afternoon, some two hours after his absence had been noticed, and the search begun. She tried to reassure me.

"I'm sure there is nothing to worry about and we'll find him quite soon but David seems to have gone off for a walk in the park. The staff are out looking for him. I'll let you know as soon as he's back."

I only heard the full story after he had been found. Then the manager of the home, having unearthed from David's past the hospital episode in the seventies, said they could not keep him in safety.

By that time I could no longer ignore the dementia dimension which sometimes, especially after many years of the disease, afflicts Parkinson's sufferers. In my own mind I referred to it as "the D-word" because I hated it so much, but with this fiasco I could no longer ignore it. When David returned to live at home, I found myself in the guiltily reluctant role of carer once again and, this time, as a carer for someone with dementia.

Why is that word so terrifying? A pause for thought and a burst of free association brings a crop of dark and powerful images readily to mind: a mad woman confined to an attic; the howls of inmates in the London Bethlehem Asylum of former times, the way the words are used in casual speech: "this place is like bedlam", "you children are driving me demented!" There are images of shame and concealment. – One remembers, for example, John, son of King George the Fifth and Queen Mary of Great Britain, kept from the public gaze in the early years of the twentieth century. – For some people the associations work below the level of consciousness, while for others they operate at a higher level of awareness. To imagine this word attaching to oneself – to yourself, or to the one you love – drags both of you down, defining you as a less-than-person, a has-been, someone whose powers are lost and – worse – forgotten as if they are or were irrelevant. It imposes a sentence from which there is no return because, as we know, at present no cure exists for dementia. Once the brain cells are dead there is no reviving them, no return from the dead of dementia.

Nevertheless in the records of the general practitioner and nurse the word is used with detachment, a medical term with no shameful, historical-cultural or emotive baggage, a matter-of-fact part of textbook terminology.

You have to ask how a term can be useful if it exists in such different ways. For all the mental health activists' attempts to rehabilitate the word, to drag it back from the darkness and terror of bedlam and the flailing arms of the asylum, to name charities after it and toss it into the conversation as if it was a mere featherweight, that D-word drops like a stone into clear water. Where the surface has been calm, that word churns up mud and stirs up trails of weed that catch, snare and drag down anyone who comes in contact with it. No wonder people steer clear of the word Dementia.

In my mind David was two persons. There was the one whom I had placed on a pedestal, had set off with on a great adventure and still held conversations with in my mind. Then there was the person I looked after in the here and now – I hoped with compassion – but who drove me wild by turning the kitchen upside down in his search for ice-cream and honey, and who needed help or an eye kept on him with every step of the day.

SPRING EQUINOX

Raki
clean naked spirit
doubt dissolver
spreading benison
in the rib cage
like a soul at song
the world becomes
generous under your
tutelage it glows
with purpose
the point is there is
a point the data are
transfigured
god is a libertarian
librarian watching the worm
writing one reading many
talking appletalk
turning water into fire
predicting score draws
& when kurdistan plays
armenia at football
in the increasing rain
you know the second
coming is at hand

March 2005
It is the 21st of March, the spring equinox, and although the clocks
have not yet moved forward to summer time, the days are longer
and lighter.

At seven in the evening it was barely dark as I stood in the
kitchen preparing my evening meal. David had eaten his early, on a
tray as usual, and I had taken him a second bowl of ice cream with
cake and maple syrup on top. On the radio, the evening news was
followed by the familiar tune announcing that perennial British
serial in a rural setting, "The Archers". I found myself tuning in
most days now, mesmerised by the story lines even though, when

my sons came down for an evening, I had to pretend I didn't mind missing it – not wishing to be labelled a sad creature.

I could see where this new Archers storyline was going and, after the visit to the doctor, Jack, despite his new vagueness could see too. It looked as if this was the beginning of an Alzheimer's theme, although the name of Alzheimer's had not yet been mentioned. You had to admit, I reflected, that the stories were well planned and the scriptwriters picked issues which were of concern to their listeners. Today Jack, the central character, was upset after his visit to the doctor's surgery; the implication of the tests he had done were clear, even to him, and he was dismayed at the burden that his wife Peggy would have to bear.

I found myself exclaiming out loud, hitting my fist into my hand. "That's it! *That's exactly it!*"

To me at this time, the words voiced the thought that had never been spoken by David. I repeated out loud, "That's exactly it!" refusing to let in the possibility of contradiction.

If David had once expressed regret about the pain that his illness was bringing on the family or had suggested that he wanted to take care of us, instead of the other way round – if that had been the case, I would have found it easier to be kind. In my embittered state of mind, disregarding any possible injustice, I reflected that that sentiment seemed not to have occurred to him. But that was the nature of the disease – or so I had been told: it made the sufferer self-absorbed and it undermined any ability to empathise with others that the sufferer might once have had.

Two days later, and the radio was on as I was getting ready for bed. You never knew what they were going to come up with to fill that night-time spot; today it was a thirty minutes air-time documentary on the subject of the psychedelic drug, LSD. I paid attention, interested to note that the first to speak – a woman and scientist – couldn't recommend highly enough the experience of taking Acid. I listened attentively to the story of the Swiss scientist, inventor of the drug. Perhaps other people knew all about this even if I didn't. But better late than never, I said to myself, as the programme continued. This Swiss scientist had made a famous "bicycle trip" after taking a dose of LSD. He cycled two and a half miles from the laboratory to his home, through the Swiss countryside, and in the course of the ride he experienced the full range of its strange effects. One speaker described the initial effect of taking the drug as, "Like a white light, a fresh canvas, enabling you to see life, and where you are." Another spoke of the effects of colours and sounds, of time slowing down, of a thrown book which seemed to travel frame by frame through the air, not just once but many times over. I was surprised to hear the voice of Aldous Huxley himself in a crackly old recording, telling the BBC that, in his opinion, LSD should be taken by professors to widen their horizons. "It would open their eyes to other types of universe," were his words. Then there was the American, whom the President of the USA labelled, "the most dangerous man in America", the first who called on people to, "turn on, tune in and drop out". LSD was banned in the USA under federal law after that.

According to another voice from the time, this was what made the Sixties culture happen in England, the trigger that released the new creativity, changing the nature of popular music to reflect the shifting moods of the Acid trip. John Lennon's "Turn off your mind" was a direct quote from his American guru, that "most dangerous man" in America.

Reflecting how closely this must have chimed with David's interests thirty years ago in the seventies, I turned the volume up and listened carefully.

The next to be interviewed spoke about the downside of the experience, bad trips, acid burn-out, lives ending in schizophrenia, "the casualties of Acid". "They pushed themselves over the brink, and sometimes they didn't return." That was the chilling part.

The programme ended with the scientist who had spoken at the beginning. Her choice of words rang a chord with me. "Blasting away all the boundaries, throwing everything up in the air...new combinations can be made, new insights, new connections, and that can be very creative."

I felt sure that this was the scene that David had inhabited, at least partially, during those Seventies years. As the final speaker said, "Once your perception's been altered, you can't really go back and pretend you didn't have that extra dimension!" Was that David? And was his different perception – the way in which he saw things differently from other people – the reason why, unaware, I had been attracted to him in the first place? Should I try and put the questions to him, I wondered, or was it really too late in his present state, and should the matter be allowed to rest? Previously when trying to pump him about drugs I had met with blank looks and a wall of non-communication, but now, armed with some names and references, perhaps there were some buttons to push.

Next day, when the moment presented itself, I took the opportunity to pose the question which, to tell the truth, had been in the back of my mind for a long time. David was looking rested, relaxed and as if his mind was receptive.

"I heard a programme about LSD last night, on the radio," I began.

He looked at me.

"About some Swiss academic who invented it...Hoffer or some name like that?

He smiled, nodding. "Hoffman," he said.

"And some famous 'bicycle trip' that he made, to get home, after he had taken it, taken LSD?"

Dave continued to smile and nod in recognition of the bicycle "trip" and enjoyment of the joke, his eyes lighting up in delighted recognition.

I continued. "And also some other guy; Leamann was it?"

"Leary," he corrected me.

"That's right, Timothy Leary. Was he a musician? An artist? Friends with John Lennon?"

"A philosopher" David told me, "Of the American variety."

"Ah."

Then the question. "So did you sometimes try it? LSD? Acid?"
– And I waited.

He nodded.

I hardly looked at him, in case he went silent just when I wanted him to continue, to tell me more about what he had got up to back then. "So what was it like? How did you find it?"

He was nodding, and smiling, walking around now with an air of reminiscence on his face and, I thought, an almost beatific smile! He continued talking.

How strange. According to the carer, before I came in from work that evening, he had been confused, agitated and inarticulate, going in and out of rooms, up and down stairs, out of the front door, and the carer had had difficulty in restraining him from going out into the street, where, she feared, his impaired mobility would get him run down by traffic in no time. Now in contrast, he was calm, smiling in a far off way and re-living those dreamlike moments.

"What was it like?" I asked.

His voice was low, weak as it usually was these days, and I found it difficult to understand.

"Say again; I didn't catch that."

"It was marvellous!"

"Marvellous? In what way was it marvellous?"

He was gesturing with wide, circular arm movements. "It made everything ... harmonious!" More gestures, conveying space, circles, colour. "It made the world ... coherent...."

"Coherent?"

"It made everything ...." – more expansive and circular gestures, with smiles of remembered enjoyment – "It made everything hold together."

I pressed him with more questions. What about the creative side of it? Had he used it to write poetry? For painting? With this group of friends, or with that group? Had the harmony and coherence lasted after the trip? But I was getting very vague responses now. I would dearly have liked to know if he had used it to make sense out of a bad situation, in other words his broken marriage, or had that not really been part of the picture?

I gestured to the two vases of colourful tulips, which stood on the table in the sunlight, in front of us, tall blooms of brilliant orange, striped with yellow. Being a few days old, their stems had adopted gracious curves and bends.

"I bet these would look wonderful if you were looking at them ....like that!"

He smiled appreciatively "Yes, amazing!"

And I smiled too. I felt I could understand.

So my guess had been correct, but would I ask him the other question, which was so important to me? Why hadn't he told me about that whole episode of his life? Would I get any sensible or reliable answer now and was it even important?

I thought it was important.

I thought that what had happened in the seventies might be the reason why we were here, and in the state we were in, now.

Yes, I definitely thought it was important that he hadn't told me.

TAMBI

Alisoun
Freckles, thin red gold hair, your vowels
with laughter living in, eyes spilled light;
the game was keep the comedy coming.

I should have talismanned you,
have you in gold, snuggling in the thin
hair on my chest, clearing a way

for those explorer occasions
when crowds were burning things
or tracer stuttered in the sky;

and this, you said, is Tambi,
my mother's publisher, and Tambi opened his
enormous memory and made a mark

smiling helplessly at the prolixity of things.

London 1972
David came out of the underground station, taking the steps two at
a time, and set off in the direction of the Harrington, the pub where
Tambi held his courts, from 11 on a Saturday morning often until
closing time, and David wanted to be the first today to buy him a
pint.

He found Tambi at the usual corner table with oceans of papers
and piles of magazines and an ash-tray already overflowing.

"Welcome my friend!" The broad face beamed and the
luminous eyes sparkled happily. "Welcome! You have been
missed." They greeted with handshakes and a thumping of
shoulders. Tambi gestured to the papers and added, "I have need of
your decision-making powers!"

"It's good to be back," David replied. "Now, first things first:
what's it going to be, Tambi? The usual?"

"Of course. How kind!" Tambi beamed his acceptance.

David returned from the bar with two pints of bitter.

"Now bring me up to date! How's progress?" And soon they were deep in discussion, Tambi leafing through poems – typed, hand-written – throwing them in the air as he searched for one in particular.

"As I said, I need your powers of discernment to help me decide. Here is a sea, an ocean of talent and the ones we choose today may decide the future direction of English literature. Is this immodest?"

"It's probably true. And modesty can go to hell!" David replied. Then, continuing on a sombre note, "And the finances? How's that going?"

Tambi shrugged expansively. "We will see it through; there is always a way. By the way," he reported, "The grant from the council came through yesterday." Then his face fell: "Ah ... but I happened to give it to the window-cleaner, who also came yesterday."

David gaped, "You gave it to...?"

Tambi hastened to explain. "He had a particular interest and I suspect a great and hidden talent for writing poetry. The money will let him get started."

Even David was taken aback, but Tambi insisted, "Inside all people there is poetry; sometimes it just takes that small gesture to bring it out. Call it what you will, the divine is in all of us. I'm sure you must agree."

David nodded and went back to looking through the poems. "There's some good stuff here. What are we doing for illustrations?"

But Tambi changed the subject. "And your lovely wife: how is she, will she not make me happy with a visit?"

David's face darkened. "It's over; she's moved out. Or rather I have."

Tambi looked concerned. "She was unhappy? Ah! The money.... She was upset?" he asked hesitantly.

"Let's just say she didn't understand."

Tambi looked contrite. David had to cheer him up. "It's alright Tambi. The magazine has to be published! Maybe I didn't explain it very well to her. Anyway, it's been coming on for some time now."

"So all this time we haven't seen you, you've been...?"

David skimmed over the question. "I've been away. Getting it sorted out. It's alright now."

Tambi nodded, looking a little happier.

"Though," David added, "I won't be able to help much with the finances right now."

"Everything will be well; we shall see." – Tambi quickly tired of talking about money.

At this point they were joined by more regulars, more of "the faithful." Chairs were pulled up, pints were ordered, and packs of cigarettes were thumped on the table for general enjoyment. A girl with red freckles brought Tambi a fresh pile of papers.

"These came today, Tambi. You have to take a look."

Then, spotting him poring over the poems, "David! You're back!"

"Ali!" he responded, "I need a light!" He waved a cigarette around in the air. "Ali come soun! And light my fire!"

She giggled. "Sweetheart I'm here. You can't believe how you've been missed. – A light for David! A match for the matchless!"

"Thanks, Ali!" David dived back into the papers. She looked disconsolate and David hugged her behind before giving her a shove.

"Soon, Ali.... Soon! Actually, if you don't mind, a bit later – OK?"

"Ali come soon," she giggled. "Is that right?"

He nodded, his mind elsewhere, by now immersed in the poems. "That's right, Ali come soon, but a bit later. OK?"

She nodded and drifted off. David had his head together with Tambi again, papers and cigarette smoke mingling in the corner of a pub in Kenzington on a mid-day in London, in 1972.

So, I reflected, Alisoun (why that spelling?) introduced David to Tambi, the Buddha of Fitzrovia, so called after another pub, the Fitzroy, which he used to frequent. But was never heard of after that. Did she just disappear? As for Tambi, the "gentleman from the Indian sub-continent". I needed to know more about him and I knew there was a book.

The volumes on the shelves in David's study were in a chaotic state: Eastern philosophy mixed with text-books on semiotics, linguistics and language-learning, studies on the Tarot jumbled up with poetry and poetry magazines, a collection of speculative works on mysticism, alternative interpretations of biblical history, early Christian heresies and volumes which had probably furnished the entire material for that block-buster *The Da Vinci* code. (Why couldn't David have written that instead of esoteric poetry? Then we would have no trouble paying for the nursing home or, even better, for a large house and a team of nurses.)

I fetched a duster with the idea that I might start to sort and put the books back into subject order. I was looking for a particular volume and happened upon it quite quickly. Laying the duster aside, I settled in an armchair with the book, *Tambimuttu*. It was a volume of tributes to a most unusual figure – a collection of poems, prose pieces, paintings and photographs. Among the names of the contributors and faces in the photographs, many were famous and familiar. I browsed, impatiently moving from one entry to another, before realising that I had to start from the beginning and read straight through. The time passed and I was drawn into Tambi's world by the compilation of tributes in the form of poems, prose and paintings which evoked an era, a milieu and a coterie from the 1940s right up to the seventies in London, New York and then London again.

London in the seventies: that would have been David's time, after Nigeria, living the literary dream and exploring the psychedelic possibilities which kicked off in the Sixties.

Tambi had certainly made a mark on David, his name occurring in conversations from time to time like a symbol of the wild, artistic life I knew David had led in London, in the years before I met him – the life I didn't know much about.

One day, in Muscat, I remembered, one of those late afternoons early in the year when the weak sun is obscured by clouds, when the wind has risen and is blowing grit and leaves in annoying swirls around the driveway and the palm tree fronds are whipping viciously, when the sea and the horizon are obscured from view and a sense of unease and dismay pervades and makes the children fractious. It was one of those days when David, returning from the office, told me, "Tambi's dead!"

I felt it had come as a blow; the death of someone important, the person who had helped him get his first poems published, but who, in recent years, David had neglected and lost touch with, as our domestic life and his own settled career changed so many things.

"Will you go back for the funeral?"

"It's over. A month ago. I've just heard."

David hardly spoke about Tambi again. Then, in England, six years later, the Tambi book arrived through the post and we read about the events that David had missed. At the Hindu Memorial service in London, there had been a photograph of his "beautiful eloquent face, wreathed in marigolds". One writer who attended has recorded her feeling that Tambi's parting gift to those present was to call to mind, "that most Indian genius of the pure spirit of ecstasy at the heart of life," which those who knew him had "recognised and responded to in him," and which he had "discerned and evoked in those poets he gathered round him in a magic circle", symbolised by the lyrebird, the "symbol of pure ecstasy", on the covers of *Poetry London*, his poetry magazine.[2]

All literary London seemed to have contributed its tributes as well as painters and poets from around the world: tributes of love and affection for an Indian Prince from Sri Lanka, son of a Catholic father who had grown up in a family whose Hindu gods and festivals appealed to him more than those of the Jesuits who educated him. There was Tambi, as one contributor described him, "dressed immaculately and fit for a prince at a posh party; and looking down-at-heel and a bit lost in a pub on Gloucester Road."[3]

As I leafed through the book, I thought I recognised scenes and the atmosphere which reigned, and where David might have fitted in; the "Hog in the Pound" and the "Fitzroy" in the heart of Tambi's kingdom of Fitzrovia. I could feel the disregard for money and where it might come from, so long as the poetry was published, and how it could have incurred the debt that had been the last straw for David's first wife. Descriptions of Tambi as "very handsome in a silver-embroidered tunic"[4] and of the poverty and squalor he lived in, "the flat with the black beetle powder on the floor, the ashtrays almost hidden under stubs, the half-finished cans of beer".[5] Then there was the launching of the poetry magazine, "so alive with ideas it made the others look colourless."[6]

One wrote of the spell he wove; "a deep inner current flowing like some great Indian river towards distant, yet-to-be-explored territory."[7] And all spoke of love and of longing for the vision of ecstasy that Tambi evoked, tantalising and out of reach, and of their regret that it had been taken away. Tambi, it seemed had been both prince of ecstasy and a man "of holy poverty".[8]

Was that what appealed to David?

Or was it:

> Drink. Drugs. Women. Death.
> Four best things to be desired.
> Four small foibles that we shared
> as the archangels of faith.
> 'Let us', we said, 'just for a joke
> experiment with experience.'[9]

This, George Barker's 'Elegiac Sonnet for Tambi' would also have had its appeal for David.

Leafing through the book I came upon one familiar name after another. Here was another – Timothy Leary. I marvelled how the threads came together!

"Tambimuttu Shines On," wrote Leary, "a transmitter of ancient wisdom and beauty," with a "Merlin sense about him that transformed the ordinary situation into something a bit magical, raised us up a level or two on the splendour dial."[10]

"A man of holy poverty." But, I thought, David knew that poverty and squalor would not have appealed to me. Was this why he kept Tambi out of our life? Or was it that Tambi represented a part of his past that he had put behind him? Whatever the reason, Tambi and that Seventies scene were clearly significant and the news of Tambi's death and funeral – and the fact he had not been there – had come as a shock. For David, Tambi had been both the person and the moment where it all came together, where passion for poetry and the promise and imminence of ecstasy had been one single form of intoxication.

Looking through the book today in the quietness of the empty house, in the study lined with the chaotic confusion of his books, I came across sentences which David had underlined in his recent shaky hand, Tambi's words: "*Poetry is the awareness of the mind to the universe. It embraces everything in the world.*"[11] Tambi – the "man of two worlds" – "heir to centuries of Hindu culture",[12] but educated in English and brought up as a Catholic. Sitting with David that afternoon I read 'Alisoun' aloud thoughtfully to him, seeing in my head the lively Ali, with the freckles and red gold hair, "vowels with laughter living in", keeping the comedy coming. I could almost hear those upper-class vowel sounds and the literary society laughter.

"So who was she – Alisoun?" ... I waited patiently.

"The daughter of Anne," he told me after a few minutes

"Anne who? Is she in here?" I pointed at the book.

He nodded. I looked through the book and found the only Anne, well-known among poets, adding her tribute to Tambi.

Tambi was dead, and David's mind was in pieces, but even so – I looked at him, smiling reminiscently and beatifically – with a touch of serenity and even, at times, of ecstasy.

BREAKOUT

Om

O Lady quiet as bone where do
you keep the spirits that you
suck?

Why must I wander to your pull?

Out of the water the armour comes
the crabs like panzers glisten on
the sand.

Whose crusade do I howl in now?

Hyenas scuttle into darkness
with their tails of shame and new
blood on their jaws.

Do I obey you even when there is
in me a sun rise and the blood
breaks in her cheeks?

Our wide eyes are waiting like the owl.

O Lady of endurance when will the
clouds open over Avalon again?

April 2005

Spring came with a rush, then went away, and now was back again.
The sun was warm and flowers in pots were coming into bloom.
On a Sunday morning I sat outside the kitchen door, basking,
secure in the knowledge that a very sleepy David was peaceful in
front of the television. Since his most recent spell in respite, when
some of his tablets had been changed, he spent the best part of the
day dozing and at weekends I made the most of my time, doing the
garden and catching up on domestic chores. I had put the box of
shoe-cleaning utensils and David's two pairs of well-worn but

favourite brown brogues out, hoping that perhaps one of the rota of carers would on an impulse take the hint. I avoided shoe-cleaning but it seemed that the carers, who were good at ironing, at hoovering when time permitted, and even on occasions at silver polishing, shared my aversion to the task. Today I would roll up my sleeves and get to work despite brown stains on hands and under fingernails; there was no rush and I might even enjoy it.

I unpacked the box finding tins of polish, brushes ("brown shine, brown polish; black shine, black polish"), dusters and odds and ends, and selected what I needed. The shoes soaked up polish like thirsty sponges and, though the two pairs of brogues were identical I noticed differences as I worked the polish in. This one, in particular was worn on the toe, not just scuffed, but deeply gouged, with the leather pock-marked and torn, so the original colour was quite lost. Plenty of polish was needed to restore any kind of surface. I worked away pleasantly, enjoying the sunshine and the rich, healthy smell of shoe-polish. A wren was singing loudly in the fir tree, ending each song with a prolonged and piercing trill, amazing for such a small creature. Collared doves were calling in the trees across the road; how, I wondered, did they produce that hollow sound, like when you blew across the top of a pipe or a milk bottle. The shoes were looking better now; the redolent polish filled the deep scuffs and restored colour and smoothness to the surfaces. I knew when the damage had been done, though I could only imagine the process. It was that day, some six weeks after the trial nursing home plan was put into action, when David had just got up and walked out. After nine hours they found him.

"Where?" I wanted to know.

"In a ditch," they told me, in the surrounding parkland. It sounded terrible.

He had gone off, or so he told them, "for an adventure", but he had fallen and had been unable to climb out. Meanwhile the nursing home had called the police, a report was given by a member of the public of a possible sighting, on the road leading to the village and also more frighteningly, to the motorway. I was telephoned only a few hours into the search. They gave me reassuring messages and I waited near the telephone. But the alarm was raised and the police helicopter was sent up: David wasn't found. When a walker reported another possible sighting, they brought in a police dog, and it was the police officer with the dog who found him. Care assistants from the nursing home had joined the search and together they got him into the police Land Rover. He told them he was thirsty and would like a cup of tea. By 7.30 in the evening he was back at the home. His hands and legs were torn and scratched by brambles and red with nettle stings, but he was otherwise unhurt. When I got to the home he was sleepy but rather serene. I wondered if he had much idea of the alarm he had caused. I myself was mortified at the resources which had been deployed and wrote my thanks, with a contribution to the Police Benevolent Fund. When people asked me where he had been found, I was reluctant to say "in a ditch", like a tramp who'd had a few too many, so I told them he had fallen into a hollow in the park and had been unable to get out.

The shoes I was working on were eloquent if silent witness of his attempts to extricate himself. Now, as I applied the polish and raised a shine, I could see how he had tried and tried again, mainly with his right foot – the left was not so badly scratched – digging the toe deep into the rough and stony side of that deep and brambly ditch. The incident had, as I was to find out in subsequent weeks, hardened the mind of the already sceptical nursing home manager about the suitability of his staying there for much longer. David meanwhile had appeared to enjoy the drama of being found, if not the trauma of fearing that he might not be.

A noise in the kitchen behind me brought me to my feet; I returned the shoe-cleaning box to its place and went to help David. He had made coffee and was about to add Fairy Liquid to it. I stayed his hand in time, offering honey instead, and carried the mug to the table in the dining room leaving him to follow, unsteadily, still only half-awake. The garden was pretty, with daffodils in the sunlight, the hedge behind beginning to turn green. We sat.

"The leaves have labels on them.... in French," he told me, looking out at the garden in an interested way. I didn't catch the rest and had to ask.

"The leaves have labels on them!" he smiled and pointed, "in French! There's a conference there."

He gestured as if it were obvious. I didn't pursue the subject but murmured an acknowledgement.

The day was too good to miss the chance of gardening; there was a rose to plant which I hoped would grow up and ramble through the old crab apple tree. Next time I came indoors I found David in the sitting-room, not asleep but, unaware of my presence, creased up with silent laughter. His gaze was upwards to the bookshelves, to the right of the fire place. I smiled with him and asked.

"What are you laughing at?"

"It's a gorilla!" he told me, and his enjoyment was plain to see. I found there was no answer to that until he turned and told me, with blue enlarged eyes, "You must remember my status!"

I was taken aback: "Status"?

"Oh, you mean your *state of mind*? The images?"

He nodded, not perturbed, it seemed, but glad I understood.

The tablets had been changed, eventually, as the psychiatrist had wished, and under supervision. The results, like these today, were not too alarming. Yes there were more spooks, but on the other hand they were less spooky, not threatening or stress-inducing as they had been in the past, but, as I could clearly see, sometimes, objects of amusement.

I recalled a conversation in the car, when David had raised the subject. Then I had called them, not spooks, but images, and had tried to explain with a mixture of science – the science as I understood and could articulate it – and literary allusion.

"As I understand it, David, something mis-functions in the brain to produce the images, one part of the brain connects to another part which it shouldn't do, and as a result it produces these images. A part of the brain which does one thing connects to a part that does another thing, so what should perhaps be sound, or memory, or touch – oh, I don't know really but that's how I see it – it comes out with an inappropriate result such as an image which shouldn't be there. And the image is real, I agree with you there, it's real in that you see the image, but the thing it represents, is actually not there, not in real terms. And so you have to banish it! Shake your staff at them, like Prospero, yes? "All spirits are melted into air, into thin air!" Make them vanish and "leave not a rack behind"!

David appreciated that. It had made some kind of sense, the science and the Shakespeare. I recalled that conversation with satisfaction.

Now the gorilla had gone and I sat with David, catching up with the Sunday papers. There was a background of television news.

TOWARDS THE SUMMER SOLSTICE

Gates
The old man leans against the gate and sucks
a gurgling furnace in his pipe.
Just two farms between him and the sky.
Behind him the bungalow's half acre of
tall grass, Koi's safari, the dog's
excited nose, and beyond the marsh,
a hump of limestone blocking out the sea.

Just the one gate. But for Koi, it's all frontier.
Clambering drystone walls, threading through
the barbed wire entangled elderberry,
and vaulting with a long dutch hoe
over the garden fencing into the cattle splat.
Hoe and dog examine the squelchy beginnings
of the marsh and find the hopping stones.

Batons of bulrush mark the deeper marsh.
Ways into the sunken lane, banks of gorse and bracken.
Lane's end. The smashed cottage. Koi and the vandals!
Gate broken, windows vacant, chimney-stack
tugged down. Fire blackened beam, remnants of a rope.
Story was: a palsy shook old William so bad
he couldn't lift a pint. Nor knock back tots of whisky.

Or spear pickled onions, or keep his dribbling back.
Bottles of beer taken at home on his garden seat
staring at the complicated oak with its elephantine
limb, the golden sickle, that pretty parasite, that sticky
birdlime coloured mistletoe. As for the tale, it mixes
well with mead, the old man chortles pubwards.

June 2005
David spent a lot of his time sleeping or snoozing. The change was
gradual. He still enjoyed the gentle outings I planned for us now
the spring weather had arrived, drives in the countryside to a

favourite view point or, on warm days sitting in the garden of the "local" with a pint on the table in front of him

Our sons came down one weekend in late May to celebrate his birthday. For David any celebration called for champagne and the drama of popping the cork, which Nigel performed. Catching the smoking liquid before it could spill over from the glasses never failed to please him. When lunch was over and David had retired to an armchair we discussed the imperceptible changes.

"I haven't really had a proper conversation with Dad for years now; not since about my first year at uni," said Joe.

"He seems to be asleep much of the time," Nigel added.

"He always used to have this poetry-reading thing at the end of lunch; do you remember that?" Nigel asked.

"Vividly!" I replied quickly. "Did you enjoy it?"

"Well, it was OK," Joe said thoughtfully. "But it was a bit much in the end. I'm not sure what it was all about. Trying to get us to like poetry?"

"We just wanted to leave the table in the end; it was a bit odd, having to sit through all that stuff. Like some Victorian father in a way," added Nigel.

"But he wasn't like that at all; not Victorian I mean," Joe protested.

"No, I think he was trying to make a point," I reflected. I think he was trying to reassert some bohemian, artistic, cultural influence into this mainly middle-England, middle-class setting. It was his way of rebelling against it."

"But he never said that – in so many words," Joe reminded us.

"For someone who wrote poetry and lived for the poets he was remarkably inarticulate," I pointed out.

"And now he can hardly talk at all!" Nigel sighed.

"I'm afraid you lost your role-model back about that time. Or it may have been a bit later, but he gave up coming to the parents' evening when you were in the upper years of Secondary. And he had always enjoyed them so much before that."

"Did he really?"

"Oh yes. He just adored talking to each of the teachers and usually hearing good stories about you both. He was so immensely proud."

"Hmm," Joe looked surprised. "I suppose he was. But he's been like this for so long now, it's hard to remember."

"And it has happened so slowly that you are hardly aware of it," Nigel added, "Like the hands of a clock; suddenly an hour has passed and you didn't notice it happening."

"And if you don't know it is happening – like we didn't – in the first place, how can you do anything about it until it's too late?"

"That is always assuming that a way to treat it and reverse the process will one day be found," Joe sighed.

As the thought struck me I put it into words: "Well, you're the scientist of the family Joe; why don't you do something about it?"

I then regretted my words as Joe snapped back.

"I don't want anything to do with it! I don't even want to think about this wretched disease which has wrecked our lives."

He sat for some time, hunched and depressed. It was the first time I had heard him express such feelings and I had thought him less vulnerable. Now there was worse to come and he went on.

"And who knows what it is going to do to us?" He paused and looked at his brother, "How is it going to affect us as well?"

"You mustn't think like that Joe," I tried to reassure him. "You simply mustn't put your own life on hold because of what has happened to your Dad."

"What has happened to him has happened to us as well; there's no getting away from it."

The two of them left in the early evening; one to catch a train, the other to meet up with friends before returning to London.

After clearing up, I sat with David as he snoozed, and I thought about what they had said. The cure – or at least treatment – for degenerative diseases of this sort seemed to be a long way off, if a possibility at all, and the route towards finding it had become divisively political. A few years ago I became involved in the debates and the campaigning that went on around the issue of stem-cell research. The subject divided opinion deeply, in particular along religious lines, and our own MP whom I wrote to, had brusquely refused to support it because of his Catholic beliefs.

I remembered a November evening in London, an evening of drizzle with wet pavements and dripping umbrellas. Wrapped up against the weather a group of twelve people was gathering outside the St Stephen's entrance to the House of Commons; only one of them was in a wheelchair, that was Martha, whom I knew a little – a fighter if ever there was one – who had been using a wheelchair for two or three years. She could manage it quite well by herself but relied on her partner to help her in crowded places and when, like today, there were roads to cross and pavements to be negotiated. Most of us were anxious and several of us were prepared to be angry. Inside we gave our names at a desk in the lobby.

It felt strange to be in this familiar setting, standing on the same spot where news correspondents give their reports on parliamentary proceedings in countless news programmes. An usher escorted us along wood-panelled corridors where heavy carpet deadened all sound. There were alcoves set into the wall at intervals, with table and chairs. We halted at one to wait for stragglers before being allowed into the committee room where the hearings were being held. The committee sat at a long table and in the chair was a Church of England Bishop whose voice I recognized from his contributions to early-morning radio. Those who had been invited to give evidence sat at the other end of the table, spoke their piece, and were questioned by members of the committee. As members of the public we had no right to speak although we did have a good view of the proceedings. Our role in being there was to demonstrate support for the research and to make sure that it was known to a wide audience through articles in newspapers, journals and publications.

We sat in wooden pews set well back from the floor of the room. It was rather like being in church, not particularly comfortable, but we could see and hear everything that was said. The debate, which has been well-documented, was around the moral and ethical principals of using foetal stem-cells in research leading towards treatments. And the point on which views diverged sharply and where I thought a satisfactory answer might never be reached, was one question. Where does life begin? – In the embryo? When the embryo becomes viable? After fourteen days? – The answer to these questions must of course determine when it becomes a crime to kill that embryo. (For the religious the question must be, When does the embryo become a soul? – "whatever the soul might be!" I thought.)

The most effective of the speakers, an eminent scientist and a skilled communicator, made it clear, in his view, that Nature itself was the greatest destroyer, squandering thousands of "unsuccessful" embryos on the way to one new life. On the other side of the argument, a Muslim cleric spoke against the research on the grounds that it went against the sacredness of life. I wondered what had happened to the pioneering spirit of enquiry that had made Muslim scholars the leaders of scientific knowledge in earlier centuries.

Six months later and on a bright morning the group assembled again at the exit of Westminster tube station. It was the day of the House of Commons debate. This time, the group was larger and included members from the special interest research group and the secretary of the national support association. But spaces inside the Strangers' Gallery were limited and many of us had to remain outside. Carrying a large placard on the train and the underground had been a challenge and aroused plenty of interest. As we assembled, there was a good dozen of us preparing to demonstrate. Once the others had gone inside to take their seats, we positioned ourselves as near to the entrance as we could and started up our noisy demonstration. Tourists looked on with interest but our main target showed up half an hour later and this was a television crew from the BBC and another from the Channel 4 News.

"Support Stem-cell Research!" we chanted, brandishing our placards and marching up and down. "Find a cure for neuro-degenerative diseases!" These were not the snappiest of slogans, but they were the messages we were determined to get across.

At first the demonstration was cheerful and good-tempered. The onlookers seemed sympathetic and the TV cameras were recording the event. Then suddenly another chant was heard, coming from a group on the opposite pavement and directed at us.

"Stem-cell research murders babies!" The repeated cry grew in intensity.

Taking advantage of a momentary distraction on the part of the two policemen on the gate, one of the group darted across and started haranguing Martha who was holding her placard high above her wheelchair. I could see he was leaning over her in an intimidating manner and taunting her. "Baby-killer, baby-killer!"

As she recoiled from him the taunting increased. "You're just a sham! The wheel-chair's a sham! Baby-killer!"

There was real anger in the man's face and real alarm in Martha's as she struggled to shield herself from the abuse he was spitting in her face.

It ended swiftly as the police moved in to separate the two groups back to their respective sides of the pavement.

As the television cameras homed in on the action, the rival group took up their chant again with new vigour. "Stem-cell research murders babies!"

We, for our part, kept up our own chant just as loud as our voices could manage. "Support stem-cell research! Find a cure for neuro-degenerative diseases!"

Later the same evening at home, having given David his tea, I switched on the evening news. I still did not know the result of the vote on the debate in the Commons. "Let's have a look, David. I want to know the result. And you might see me if you're lucky!"

David nodded happily. Did he understand what the debate was all about? I wasn't sure. And even if the legislation did go through, such research was unlikely to be of benefit to David.

As the news came on, I held his hand, gripping it harder than necessary in my anxiety. Yes! The vote had gone the way we wanted and the research would continue. Some scenes from the debate were shown, before the correspondent reported on the scene outside.

"Ugly exchanges took place on the pavements outside the House between those in favour and those against, while inside MPs voted to allow the controversial research to continue...."

"Look David – there's that horrid man – just look at him, actually spitting at Martha! Oh, and there's me! Just behind her!"

David was smiling and patting my hand. "Well done! Clever girl! Well done!"

And he raised his glass to me, as if the vote of Parliament had been entirely my own achievement.

There was more work to be done. Another crucial debate and a vote were scheduled for the European Parliament, and both the national committee and the local branch urged us all to write letters

– they almost wrote them for us. The work went on, bringing the hoped-for cure nearer. Even if it wasn't going to benefit David, it gave me satisfaction to be part of it and relieved some of the frustration.

As I handed him his six o'clock tablets, the oval-shaped yellow ones that supplied the regular dose of *leva-dopa* without which he would be immobilised most of the time, I had to remember that David was indeed benefiting from research carried out in earlier decades, which had uncovered the role played by dopamine in carrying the orders of the brain to the parts of the body which it controlled.

On that May evening I brought David a cup of tea and sat with him. He took a variety of tablets through the course of the day and I wondered whether, in the days before I had taken charge of them, he had simply had too much medication. His attitude to the medication following the diagnosis of Parkinson's seemed to have become "more is better" and, even after I had taken over, it was some time before I became convinced that the opposite should be the case. To keep him mobile and moving had seemed, back then, the all-important aim, and, if that meant more tablets, we had moved the dosage up a step, never without the consultant's agreement, but he wasn't difficult to convince. It was only after the spooks appeared on the scene, which the medication appeared to be responsible for, that some changes were made and even then yet more tablets were brought in to repel the invaders. And now those tablets were under suspicion. Could it be that they had been responsible for the deterioration of his mental faculties? Had I been slandering David with my speculations about acid trips in the seventies? I would never know and would have to accept this fact. People asked why David hadn't gone for surgery, deep brain stimulation and the other innovative treatments. But the medics had not been in favour and, in my view, David would never have risked someone poking wires into his brain – that would have been too much. Current research looked promising and, within ten or twenty years, I realized, the outlook could be entirely different.

I looked at him, snoozing in his chair, and wondered again where it all started and where it was all going. A fly buzzed around, irritatingly, trapped between the window and the double-glazing: one of those flies which come awake when the sun warms them, buzzing infuriatingly in inaccessible corners; this one was well and truly trapped. It had my sympathy and I went in search of a glass tumbler and a sheet of paper. With great care, I retrieved the fly and put it outside to enjoy its freedom in the great outdoors. Surely if all life was sacred, as the protesters claimed, it didn't apply only to humans? Perhaps, I thought, I should call myself a Buddhist, like the holy men who sweep the ground before they walk on it, to spare the lives of ants.   And would the ants be there in heaven? Strictly speaking, Christians don't believe animals have souls, do they? And I imagined that Muslims felt the same. So there wouldn't be any in heaven. I felt that I couldn't appreciate a heaven where there wouldn't be any animals. And why shouldn't they have souls? The discussion went on inside my head.

When had I last had a good discussion with David? Really not for years, if I was honest. And I remembered him again as he had been, questing, enthusiastic, dynamic. As for soul, what version of David, along the course of his trajectory, was the version which was going to survive after him? What version of anyone, for that matter? What version of myself would I want to survive into the after-world?

If you saw life as a story, overlapping with the stories of other lives, if you saw it that way, I reflected, you could keep some degree of control over its direction. But then, simply by interacting with other lives, you voluntarily forfeited some control. It's when there is no story, when nothing happens and the narrative ceases to evolve, I thought, that life becomes unbearable. That's one reason why heaven must be a dull place for, where time ceases to exist, stories become impossible: no day-by-day unfolding of events, no waiting, no wondering, "What next?" No more stories.

David was more alert now: time for another cup of tea.

MAKING THE MOVE

Holly Bush Lane (*fragment*)
Dr Parkinson I presume? And your gallery
of slow, glacially slow, characters.
the utter eerie peace. Patience on a monument. Sheer stasis.

I bring you spasms and paralysis in broken language
stuttering locked into spluttering syllables.
You talk of dopamine, acetylcholine
messengers of control of movement.
A shortage of these stiffens muscles,
Mineralises them, delivers motion slow as
Glistering slugs, tremors on lips and hands,
Blurred double vision...

Strangers grazing in your semantic fields.

February 2006
The carer had labelled the shelves in David's study with neat tabs:
"Philosophy", "History", "Linguistics", "Semiotics". They looked
good for a time but David soon jumbled them up and seemed
happy for them to remain that way. Philip Pullman's novels had
appealed to him and stood alongside a classic on the Cathars of
medieval France, essays on Pragmatics and "The Loom of
Language", "The Language of Metaphor", the "I Ching" and "The
Lives of John Lennon", filling the shelves in random order.
Recently David had read each Harry Potter volume as it came out,
underlining the bits that took his fancy.

Life was becoming a little like the nursery, with rituals
dominating the day, the chief of them being the timetable of
medication. As David found it hard to pick up the tiny tablets I
would hold them to his lips, and he accepted them like a
communicant receiving the wafer from the priest. And being child-
like didn't seem to bother him too much; I noted how the attentions
of the daily carers were received without any show of
embarrassment, indeed with pleasure and enjoyment at being at the

centre of their kind attentions; if anything the embarrassment was in my own mind.

Conversation would have been nice, in the evenings when I came back from work and after the carer had left. I craved meaningful interaction, the way mothers with small children long for adult conversation. David retired for bed at 7.30 nowadays and my routine was to help him through to the bedroom, negotiate the business of the bathroom and get him undressed and into bed. After that I would unwind, making a meal for myself. But before I could do that, David needed his book and, with the power of speech almost gone at this stage of the day, the puzzle was to know which book he meant.

"This one?" I offered him *The English Imagination*, the book he had been browsing through during the day.

A shake of the head.

"So which? Tell me!" I coaxed.

David fumbled for the name: "Larry Farmer."

"I'm sorry?"

He tried again: "Wally Harper". He paused and then again: "Harri-parri".

By this time anxiety at the effort of getting it right and getting it out was showing on David's face. This was no joke, but a serious business and I soon got the message.

"Here you are – the 'Harry Potter'!" I handed it to him and saw him relaxed and beginning to doze off, with the book in his hands.

What was he thinking about, I often asked myself. "Thinking" must be the wrong word. What was going on in his head? What thoughts were taking place? In what confusion of disorder? Was it like clouds swirling around, sometimes forming into sensible shapes? I knew that at times his mind was clear and he could express himself and interact, in however limited a way, and in the earlier part of the day it was always better. It wasn't as if he failed to recognise people – at least the people he knew well – he had always been bad at remembering slight acquaintances. If you asked him what the TV news had been about he might have little to say, but if you asked him about works of classic literature, the rules of cricket or some branch of linguistic theory, or any of the subjects which had burned their way deep into his mind, he would relax and appear – even if his contribution was superficial – to be on familiar territory.

What went on in his mind, I wondered, after I had left him for the night? When he woke in the depths of the night? And what thoughts occurred in the early morning before I was around? What thoughts were going through his head as he watched the TV news, or the cricket or the tennis in the afternoon? It really bothered me that I could not understand and that I had no access to his thought-processes. I read up about neuroscience and about synapses and receptors, plasticity and the process of learning in children, how the brain compensated and sometimes recovered when injury occurred. David had thought about it and there were books on his shelves to prove it. He knew about dopamine deficiency in Parkinson's, that shortage of chemical messengers which, he had written, "...*stiffens muscles,/ Mineralises them, delivers motion slow as/ Glistering slugs, tremors on lips and hands,/ Blurred double vision...*", and equally he knew about hallucinations, those, "*strangers grazing in your semantic fields*".[13]

That was his last poem – the last he would ever write – even though, when doctors asked if he was still writing poetry, he would nod and tell them Yes.

Apart from that, David hardly spoke to me about his condition, so how could I gauge how he felt about it emotionally? Thus I assumed the worst but admitted to myself that possibly by now he didn't feel emotion sharply. Emotionally it was I who did the feeling ... and the fuming.

There were plenty more rituals, some for him, some for me, others for the carers who came in the daytime. I listed them mentally.

First the ritual of laying out the tablets each evening for the next day. Six little compartments held the tablets, to be given at two-hourly intervals, from eight in the morning till six at night. After that, the preparation of the pump, the tiny pump that fitted inside David's breast pocket – "Never buy shirts without breast pockets", I had to remind myself – which delivered the medication that supplemented the tablets which had been laid out in the box with the six small compartments. Check that the syringe, the butterfly line, the special adhesive strip that kept the needle in place, were all ready for setting up in the morning. Next, before I went to bed, give him the night-time tablets and settle him for the night.

Then there were the rituals that marked the weeks and the months: the weekly visit from the district nurse to fill the supply of syringes, check for pressure sores and anything else that might be a problem. At other intervals there were calls from the chiropodist, the hair-dresser, the team of ladies with the mobile library. These were regular events which kept David busy and warranted a mark on the calendar by the day-time carers who kept an eye on the week's routine.

And how did the carers cope? I had only to look in their record book to know how the days passed: the notes were kept with detailed accuracy, the fact that this was required by the agency that sent them and the inspectors who inspected the agency in no way concealed the caring attention that they provided, for which I was profoundly grateful.

6th December. A wash today – David didn't feel like a shower. Tea and cake at 10.30 am. Library ladies visited to renew books and cassettes. Listened to a rousing Beethoven CD, David very relaxed after conducting his way thro the CD.
10th December. David had a shower today. In an extremely good mood and very mobile so was able to dress himself. Settled to watch cricket. After lunch mobility poor again
14th December. Shower and shave today. Blister on left thigh sore-looking but dry; antiseptic cream applied.

That was before Christmas. Now, once again, we are preparing for him to move to a nursing home. This time it will probably be permanent. We have been careful; David has visited the home, along with myself and with the carer whom he most trusts, but it is a most painful time. I spend my days torn in two but recognising that we are moving unremittingly along those lines, and putting in place, one by one, the financial arrangements to deal with the situation. I have organised a team of advisers around myself and set up an annuity that will supplement David's pension to pay for care. It will involve selling the house, but this – happily – can be deferred for a year. The enduring power of attorney was dealt with a year or more ago when the specialist psychiatrist was able to talk

David gently through its contents to make sure he understood what he was signing.

In between the practicalities, I wonder what the carers think: are they telling themselves that I have finally given up? But they're far too professional to say anything of the sort and continue to give support in all the practical details, to David and also to me.

Carers' notes

8th February. *Sat and chatted to David, held his hand. Talked about the nursing home and how spring was a good time of the year for moving and "new projects". He agreed. David wrote his name in some of the books he's taking with him. Sewed more name-tapes into clothes which will go with him.*

13th February. *Shave, shower and hair-wash today. David quite confused during his shave and getting dressed. This improved after a 5 minute nap on the bed. He took his cup of tea and walked around the garden. Came in and settled to read/doze. After lunch David chose some framed photos and pictures and tarot cards that he wanted to take with him. I polished/dusted them and put them on table for Sarah to pack. ... Sewed name labels onto more clothes.*

15th February. *A wash for David today. Pharmacy called to deliver David's medications. David very agitated this morning, asked me to telephone Sarah, which I did and left a message. ... Washing on. Ironing done. Sewed more name labels on clothes. Labelled videos David is taking tomorrow. Assisted David to choose CDs to label and take. Trimmed and cleaned David's fingernails. District nurse called to say goodbye to David.*

16th February. *Shave, shower and hair wash today. Packed David's things to go to nursing home this afternoon. Bed linen washed. Ironing done.*
Sarah and I took David to nursing home.

That was it: the move was made. I was home by tea time – in bed by ten.

I woke in the middle of the night. Guilt hit me with the force of a blow to the stomach and the intensity of a supernatural revelation.

What had I done? I felt sick. How could I have gone through with it? What could I possibly do now to change it?

Doubt and despair were so strong I could not stay still, I had to get up, move about. I put on the light, stood up, sat down, held my head in my hands and groaned. I had thought I would have felt relieved, free, able to relax. How could I live with this?

I went downstairs, made tea, moved around; I felt the cold and shivered, but anything to numb the pain and the sickness in my stomach.

Back upstairs, I climbed into bed again. Exhausted and drowsy I looked for a book and picked up the nearest: Harry Potter was the one that came to hand.

FOOL ON THE HILL

The Dreamer
asleep on his owl faced sheep
the dreamer
mediates for us
an almost Turkish moon
aureoled above the frail trees
& the blank
faced house

in his dream he
is over the moonlicked
stile
& staring back
at the blank blank house
you will not hold me
either in this body
or that

stooks of corn
suck the darkness
into their stalks
& climbing through earthskin
into moonhair
like a spine flowering skull
the tree tells
the journey is the same

March 2006
After a few weeks at the nursing home a routine established itself.
This home was so much better and more suited to David's needs
than the one we had tried with disastrous outcome two years ago. I
visited midweek and weekends; midweek I would sit with him,
arriving in time for the afternoon trolley of tea and cakes.
Weekends, either Saturday or Sunday, I would take him out for
lunch: one local pub was quiet and friendly and the gay couple
who ran it were understanding. David still relished holding a pint

in his hands and eating a plate of fish and chips. I bought the Sunday papers and the pub garden was a good place to look through them, talk to David about the cricket scores and tell him news of friends and of Joe and Nigel. After lunch we would go for a drive and I would chat about the weather and the signs of the changing seasons. David's mood varied; sometimes he seemed settled enough, but returning to the nursing home and saying goodbye were always difficult and at these moments I tried to get one of the care assistants to be with him, to lift his mood if necessary. With David's impassive face it was hard to tell what he was feeling, so that sometimes I wondered if the emotion I detected in him was really all inside myself. There were days when I drove away relieved and light-hearted that he was settled and well cared for and, having done my midweek duty, I could escape and get on with my plans. Because there was no denying that it was a duty. Driving fifteen miles and back twice a week to entertain him, reassure him, show that I was still there for him and keep him in touch with family life, was hard, as well as judging just how much to talk about my own life and the business I was running, which must have seemed quite pointless and devoid of interest to him. Did he ever wonder why I was doing it? I wanted to reassure him that everything was fine, and not let on that, financially, I felt far from secure.

Sometimes I would bring him home, for Sunday lunch. I could sense him enjoying the familiar rhythms of cooking and eating together and afterwards sitting outside in the sunshine. Once or twice he stayed overnight but taking him back to the home was always that much more difficult, and the torment of guilt kicked in again, despite knowing that it had to be this way.

I now had to sell the house and find somewhere new to live, somewhere suitable for living on my own but roomy enough for Joe and Nigel to feel at home when they came for weekends, and where David could come from time to time. Perhaps things would be easier once this was completed.

When it came to the point of selling, David's financial sense was still sufficiently alive to register his pleasure; he positively beamed on learning that we had made a good sale, good enough for me to buy a place I would enjoy rather than the "box" that I had warned my friends I was going to live in.

Bringing David to the new house, however, was another hurdle. Would he understand? Or would he think that he was to return and live there too? Would he be confused coming to a different house and how should I refer to it? As "home"? Whose home? As "our house" or "my house"? In the end I usually talked about "the house" and left it at that.

After David had been in the nursing home for a few months, to my surprise I found there were occasions to enjoy, like when our friend Colin came down to visit and the three of us could be together. I usually arranged for us to meet somewhere near the nursing home for lunch and beers. The two men greeted each other in the old familiar style, a slap on the shoulder and shaking of hands, Colin providing more than the usual warmth, aware of how much David needed the physical contact of a warm embrace to replace the jocularity and exchange of banter which he could no longer deal out. As we progressed with the meal Colin and I maintained the conversation, with David included as a non-speaking participant. It worked.

And there were other good moments for David, provided by the staff of nurses and carers in the home. I could see how relationships were gradually developing between David and the staff. While he hardly spoke to other residents, he related in gentle ways to the people who looked after him, and in ways that I found surprising. The person whom I had first known as impatient, energetic, frequently abrasive, now became known for his gentleness, his warmth and humour, which the staff enjoyed and liked to tell me about: like the nurse who returned from holiday:

"When I came back I said 'Hello David, have you been good?' and, quick as a flash, he came back with, 'Have I been God? – Yes, that's right – 'God!' – We loved it!"

Few among the residents were able to lighten the day for their carers like that and many were confused and angry to such an extent that I had to admire how the staff kept their kindness and humanity and their own good humour. On one particular afternoon I arrived for a visit only to find my way barred by a resident who was claiming David for herself!

"That's my husband," she told me in loud tones. "I'm sorry but he is my husband – you can't go in there!" Eventually a carer came to the rescue, taking the lady off for a cup of tea.

While David communicated only with staff, some of the residents did relate to each other and I could see that gradually they were turning into a community. I began to recognise patterns, certain ladies who sat together, feeling comfortable in each other's company, exchanging words. You couldn't really call it having conversations together, more like exchanging words in a script, which they shared and recognised. What were the scripts based on? Perhaps on a similar upbringing, maybe on the experiences of life shared by a generation.

Among the staff many were from other countries and cultures. I was surprised at how well they were able to communicate with people whose speech was frequently chaotic, brought to a standstill by the obstinate refusal of synapses to transmit the thought in the head to the lips that urgently wanted to speak it. How did they learn to do this work when their own grasp of the English language was basic, to say the least?

Where did David fit into this spectrum of disabilities? I knew that there were times when he simply could not get his thoughts into words, whilst at other times it appeared as if the script was there, while the thought was somehow missing. He would start off with energy on a favourite theme from the past. "So! We'd better arrange a meeting for...." And then he would trail off into inarticulacy. I recognised a formula from the old days, usually towards the end of a phone conversation or an office meeting, triggered here by who knows what?

At other times I saw him plunged deep in a no-man's land of discomfort and confusion, visible in the lines in his face. But even then, when something urgent had been brewing in his consciousness over days, at such times he would take me by surprise with words pronounced in a low and weak voice but all the more forceful for that. Like the afternoon in early December as we sat together, when he said quietly, "I want to be at home for Christmas."

And Christmas with family gatherings brought David to life. Now he could not join in conversation, since his power of speech had so significantly declined, but his enjoyment was in being part of the group. As I watched his face I could see the animation inside him and, when he tired of paying attention, the relaxation that came over his face. If only every day could bring such highlights and make life worth living.

A year passed. January and February were difficult months but March arrived and one sunny afternoon, with spring in the air, I arrived to take David for a drive. I had brought the wheelchair to transport him to the car but, disappointingly, found David slumped in a day room, head bent forward, his face masked, drawn and pained and no carer in attendance. I sat down with him.

"Shall we go out? It's a lovely afternoon; let's get out there!" I didn't want to change my plans but David was glacial and his limbs refused to move. I tried to get him going.

"Come on, put a hand here. No, here, like this! And your right leg here; here! Come on David, like this!" Somehow, without calling for help, I manoeuvred him to the wheelchair. From there I could get him to the lift and so downstairs and out to where the car was parked. I wheeled the chair forward and opened the passenger door.

"Now: up you get ...that's right. Sit in here....bottom first...."

And at this point, not for the first time, old habits kicked in. That familiar movement of getting, seat first, into a car and swinging the legs in afterwards, was so engrained that David's auto-pilot took over. I protected his head, feeling yet again that pigeon's egg of a bump –the one acquired from the falling garage door in Germany years ago, and I saw that from this stage the movement was automatic. Soon he was seated and I had fastened his seat belt. The wheelchair was stowed in the boot and we were underway.

David's face, however, was still drawn, tense and pained and I knew it would take a while for him to relax and engage. I performed my routine: put the cassette into the player, change gears and swing out into the afternoon traffic. It was a mile or more, through a busy high street onto the main road and a wait at the traffic lights, before we could get off onto the side roads which led to woodlands and countryside. I glanced at David anxiously as the traffic lights held us up. Happily the music had started, working its magic, and transformation was taking place. As strong and familiar rhythms and words filled the car, the pained expression, the tension and the deep lines eased from his face. Next time I glanced at him David was smiling, conducting with one hand and slapping his knee with the other to strains of Strawberry Fields. It was as if the pain and confusion had simply melted away and had never been; David was beaming, nodding, enjoying the show: "Let me take you down, 'cos I'm going there, to Strawberry Fields, nothing is new." I joined in and we sang it together. "Strawberry Fi –e –lds for ever!" And again on a rising note, "Strawberry Fields for ever!"

The traffic lights turned to green: up the hill and turn right at the junction, diving now into the leafy tunnel that leads over the Chart, the high woodland plateau with its far-reaching views to distant hills beyond. Things were improving: sunshine poured through the canopy of trees and to our right vistas of the High Weald stretched into blue southern distance and were accompanied by triumphal northern brass trumpeting: "Penny Lane... is in my ears ...and in my eyes." Together we joined in, I at full volume, David more weakly but conducting with both hands and head held high: "Here...beneath the blue, suburban skies ... I ...." We ran out of the words and hummed and tra-la-ed along, joining in at full throttle as the joyful trumpet solo rang out, carrying the words along, diminishing into a quiet and reflective, "Penny La-a-a-ne".

Sergeant Pepper came next and we belted it out together: "Sergeant Pepper's Lonely – Sergeant Pepper's Lonely – Sergeant Pepper's Lonely – HEARTS – CLUB –BAND!!"

I was smiling now too, enjoying the moment. I looked across and patted David on the knee as we waited for the next number. The road was downhill, winding towards a village where we turned left into a small country lane.

"Hey Jude" and "The Long and Winding Road" followed each other on the cassette.

As David strummed with one hand on his knee I was transported to Muscat 1986. Two small boys and a 4x4 loaded with camping gear, cold boxes with food for the weekend and cold drinks, everything needed to cope with temperatures in the 40s Celsius. We were with friends in convoy, heading for our favourite spot, a rare place with a running stream amid the rocky valleys, and pools, where the water was cool even in the heat of a blazing mid-day sun. We always chose a weekend when there was a moon and at night the shadows cast by the cliffs and rocks made strange shapes and the silence, after the generator of the far-off village had finished its work for the evening, was absolute. Then, on the return journey, threading along red earth tracks and bumping over pot-holes, checking familiar landmarks in the rocks to ensure we were on the right track, joining the hard-top road back to the city it was "The Long and Winding Road" which accompanied us.

That track ended and I jolted back to the reality of the country lane as a red sports car closed into the rear-view mirror and there was not much room to let it pass. I pulled in to a field gateway to let it by. The Winding Road had been succeeded by "Hey Jude" and I was still in the Gulf.

"Do you remember the detour we did that day after camping?" I asked David. "The village where the wedding was going on? We had 'Hey Jude' on. It was keeping the boys happy in the back of the Range Rover."

David nodded but I had no way of knowing if he remembered or was doing it for the sake of our shared enjoyment. Whichever way, it didn't matter…this was a pleasant moment.

As we wound our way along the twisty road, I pointed out where bluebells were coming into flower and hawthorn hedges were greening up. David nodded compliantly.

Now it was "Can't Buy Me Love". We picked up the rhythm together, I thumping the steering wheel, David waving and nodding his head from side to side. I pulled the car up at the side of a lake, the object of the drive, parked and, leaving David with the tape still playing, I got out to stretch my legs and enjoy the scenery.

When I got back, the tape had ended and David had dozed off. I gave myself another ten minutes to walk in the sunshine, then shared a bar of chocolate when David woke up.

The second Beatles tape accompanied us on the way back, less loudly this time, but we still joined in. We beat time to "Back in the USSR", followed gently and reflectively by a favourite of David's "The Fool on the Hill". Then "Yellow Submarine", which David thumped along to, brought us with perfect timing back to where we had started.

"Did you have a nice time?" the carer who helped us in asked. David smiled and agreed that we had and that a cup of tea and cake would be nice.

We had, indeed, had a nice time and in acknowledging the fact I accepted the wisdom of enjoying such times and not hankering after the past.

NOTHING IS ACCIDENTAL

Towards The Feast (*Ethiopia 1969*)
The kettle sellers beat
the darkness into their mules
This morning is holy

The yeast slow dawn
bubbles in the lope of carriers
their heels escaping the sticky world
as the toes knead in

They know the earth sucks
that's why the laterite is red

The basalt pushes out its heads
They do not watch the procession
swingeing on horseback at sheep
arse under yoke load up the hill
They are on a long black trip

The sun trembles like a new dropped foal
God nailed, a spear in his side. A twist
of thorny crown. Mary with her chalice
catching the thinning clumps of blood

And everywhere the hungry light

May 2007
A year passed for David at the nursing home and I was getting my
life back or at least establishing some sort of equilibrium.

"I've been asked to go to Ethiopia," I told David on one of my
visits. "It's a kind of consultancy...." I gave him time to take in
what I had said and to react. "What do you think? Do you mind?" I
held my breath; I had already said I would go; would he feel
bitterness, that the projects which he used to get sent on were
coming my way now? Would he feel upset that I would be going
so far away, leaving him, abandoning him? "It's only for a few

weeks actually, I won't be gone long." His response, which was a long time coming, was a smile of low-voiced approval: "Very good!" I breathed out and squeezed his hand.

"I'm going to read you the poem: do you remember 'Towards the Feast'?" He nodded. When I had finished it I asked "Do you remember where you wrote that? Where was the feast?" I hardly expected him to recall it but the answer came back straight away:
"Dire Dawa!" It was one of the towns on my itinerary and the poem would make it significant. Strange how things seemed to be tying up – coming together: was it accidental?

Lalibela, Ethiopia, July 2007

So here I was: a hilltop town in 2007. By the Ethiopian calendar it was still 1999 and visible preparations were being made to let the world know that Ethiopia was about to celebrate the new era, six years and seven months after the rest of the world. I had already discovered that in Ethiopia they do things differently. This must have suited David down to the ground in the late 1960s, when he had spent three years as a teacher in the largest secondary school in the country. I had never learnt much from David about his time there: yes he had taught English: he had produced plays – that was the best thing, even putting them on in the city's National Theatre. And in his spare time he had travelled and seen the country, writing travel articles for the national tourist board. No, in answer to my questions, he had never gone back. So little nostalgia for a place he had spent three years in surprised me. For myself, I always felt the necessity to revisit a country, once at least, to lay to rest the memories – "laying the ghost" I called it – but not David. Leave and move on seemed to be his rule of thumb. What brought those years to life for me one day, was a phone call and a visit from a student of his from those days. Affectionately calling David, "the Master", refugees from political turmoil – the nut-brown Professor Tadele, writer and teacher of English himself now, and his wife – came and stayed and helped us with the apple harvest and cooked strange food – which delighted our two boys – and brought gifts of coffee beans, which they roasted and brewed to an inky black sweetness. I knew vaguely that they were Christians in Ethiopia and invited them to attend the village church, which they did rather shyly, and I was acutely embarrassed that the congregation stood back stiffly and failed to welcome them warmly. They were on their way to Poland where perhaps the welcome would be warmer: this was pre 1989 and socialists from Africa were welcomed in communist Eastern Europe.

That was nearly twenty years ago, and in a hilltop town in the Ethiopian highlands I was only now able to appreciate the shocking contrast which the professor and his wife must have felt between our easy comfortable life and where they had come from.

Once the business side of the trip was completed, I had been determined to visit some of the places where David would have gone in the late 1960s. Much was different from what I had expected, like the round churches where the priests guarded the holy of holies and I saw paintings of bible stories quite different from the versions I was familiar with. Even the way they told the time was different here, which was causing me great confusion.

I had visited the rock-hewn churches and watched the sun set over the mountains from the balcony of the "Jerusalem Guest House" where I was staying. As darkness fell and a crescent moon rose, from the houses in the street below a murmur of voices swelled and, although it was dark, the smell of smoke fires and clattering of cooking pans, barking of dogs, and voices of children, described the scene which I could not see.

That had been my last full day and the following morning a minibus would be waiting to take me and others to the airport, twenty-five kilometres away down in the plain. I didn't want to miss it or miss the plane.

As the driver negotiated a way out of the town, there were crowds which had not been present the day before. "Is market today in Lalibela," the driver told us, looking at his watch – he too was worried about being late for the plane. Even after we reached the edge of the town, there was no lessening of the crowd coming to market, and with a jolt I felt myself drop back to the scene that David had described in the poem. I was seeing it for myself, the people making their way eagerly to the market – to the feast. They were coming in their thousands – lean, spare, wiry, clothed in homespun shirts and shawls, staves in hand, driving donkeys, goats, sheep to the market, laden with bundles, men and women, children too. These were not the starving figures that television reports in the 1980s had showed or, if there were among them the survivors from those awful days, their children were here too. For several kilometres we threaded our way slowly down and round and round and down the mountainous road, slowly against the tide of men, women and children, donkeys, sheep and goats, chickens hanging upside down from poles slung across backs, it seemed more like a migration, a cheerful migration for there were smiles and anticipation on the faces and excitement in the air. For some ten kilometres they kept coming, striding out and taking short-cuts up steep mountainside to cut off the winding bends. How far had they come? Had they set out in the darkness, before the "yeast slow dawn"? I had no idea what feast they were heading for, but there was in their faces the sense, as David had written, that, "This morning is holy".

And I had come all this way too – to discover the meaning of one more poem. How much of an accident was that?

A GLASS BOX OF TIME

The Coming Of Rhiannon
Once in a glass box of time
the prince of sense & caution
held his court.

To him the scene was clear
skulls were opening
visions in the air

There was the hollow hill
with Boadicea's breast
on offer to the sky;

here was the court
with its plots,
placemen, plunder.

Inside the crystal box
the symbolist with stave and globe
making, unmaking signs.

He smiles. The mapmaker
is of course himself and all
these blurred images

are signs still loose
like nets without knots,
like the incomplete

blundering in the underworld
creating such farrago as
a storm of untufted eyes.

He has learnt much of
signs during his year
and a day away,

and here in this ventricle, this
chamber, this rope route
to the undertree,

this prince of sense and caution
takes a second wager
on the coming of Rhiannon.

The nursing home, June 2007

Summer rain lashed the roads as I drove to visit David. No thought
of going out today. I had brought him chocolates and he helped
himself with enthusiasm and, now that I was there with him, he
relaxed, stretched out upon the bed.

"I've brought some sewing," I told him. "I'll just get on with it."
I pulled the spare chair up to the side of the bed so I could hold his
hand and with the other emptied the contents of a bag. Scissors, a
needle-case made of felt with a cut-out cockerel stitched only
slightly askew on the front. This must have been the first fruits of
the very first school term of – now was it Joe or Nigel? – Irritating
that I could not remember which of them had produced this
treasure! Some printed cotton material – Laura Ashley with its
sprigs and flowers – I had bought it at a village fete. What should I
make with this leftover? David was relaxed to have me here,
sewing and chatting intermittently, exclaiming when I made a
mistake, or swearing when I pricked a finger. The walnut wood
sewing-box was a lucky-dip of memories. I let my mind wander as
I rummaged for some binding to go with the Laura Ashley. This
could be just right, the right colour – rick-rack binding didn't they
call it? There were buttons in a cardboard chocolate-box, pins in a
box marked, "Dorcas", lace, removed from nightdresses, lengths of
elastic with no "give" left in them, hooks and eyes, poppers, glove-
stretchers, a vial of smelling-salts which I had once made the
mistake of putting to my nose and inhaling. – Enough to have
awoken the dead! – Who had that belonged to? In this tranquil way
the time passed, pleasantly.

David stirred.

"Look! I've done all this!" I held up my sewing.

He smiled and attempted to prop himself up.

"Have these pillows!" I helped to get him upright. "Shall I read?"

He nodded.

"It's *The Mabinogion*. I found it in a bookshop – a new English translation."

David reacted with a warm smile; he was alert now, ready to hear. He had used these old Welsh tales as an inspiration for many of his own poems.

"It's the one where they go to Ireland," I told him. And, with my best Irish accent, "Would you be ready now?"

I hadn't paid much attention back then, although I had known that the poetry he was writing called on the Welsh tales. Writing poetry was what he did whilst the rest of us followed our own pursuits. With his disease kicking in, with judgement failing and that dynamic energy – which had planned and scheduled and worked to deadlines – failing fast, I had to pick up the pieces where he could no longer manage; whether running the household finances, attending parents' evenings without him, or helping the children with decisions on their choice of studies. To them poetry was just "something that Daddy did", and although it now seemed unlikely, I had little time then to pay it much attention. With hindsight I appreciated and wondered at that flourishing of creativity, even as the disease crippled his other faculties, so when I had come across this new translation of the tales of Pwll, Haroun, and Rhiannon, I bought the book and resolved to read the stories for him – perhaps to make amends, but with enjoyment too.

Three in the afternoon: and a carer with a trolley brought tea and cakes.

"Would you like it here or do you want to come to the dining-room?"

"We'll have it here – thank you!"

Outside the rain was slackening but the sky was still overcast. The view of the North Downs was obscured by mist and thin drizzle. We were best inside and warm and protected, reading stories of heroes on this wet afternoon.

In the Island of the Mighty, heroes with unpronounceable names were carousing with the King of Ireland. I adopted the best broad Irish accent I was capable of to make him laugh and together we enjoyed the tale: "The Irish," I read, "had a cunning plan" – that familiar Black Adder phrase made us both laugh – and I read the story. It told how the Irish placed men in bags and hung them from pegs. The Welsh came along and asked what was in the bags: "Flour, friend!" they were told. Three times it was repeated – my accent broader and David's smile cracking wider with each repetition until the wily Welsh outwitted the cunning Irish and both sides sat down together to feasting and carousing. More treachery followed, with fighting, beheadings and feasting in Harlech for seven years, with the birds of Rhiannon singing along.

"What day is it?" David asked me. He was living in that glass box of time now, stepping outside for intervals when I visited, and, I liked to think, glimpsing the world outside through my mediation, content perhaps to read the reflections, to listen through me and those around him to echoes of the people of a former life, and to absorb the attention and care from those who attended him in the undoubtedly comfortable surroundings. My visits were highlights. Usually the staff knew I was coming and he was prepared to see me, shaven and trim and well-dressed as he always liked to be. But occasionally when I arrived I found him sunk into himself, not conscious of anything going on around him.

Months passed, summer turned to autumn. The routine of visiting, going for drives, continued, with David's mind sometimes with me, sometimes somewhere else.

How did you get inside the mind of a man with dementia? I thought about it continually: what was going on in there? I knew that it was by no means always a blank; much of the time David interacted with the nurses and the carers, as I could tell from what they told me. The new girl, Anna, when I introduced myself as David's wife, told me, "Such a lovely man – we love him!"

But there must be long periods of confusion: what was that like? A muddle of crossed wires, a skein of mixed up ideas? A low and monotonous buzz?

Xxxxxxxxxkkkkkkkkkkkkzzzzzzzzz..........zzzzzzzzzzchchchchchj jjjjjjjjjjkkkkkkkkkzzzzzzzzzzzzzzzzzzzzzzzzzchchchchchxxxxxxxxxxxz zzzzz..........zzzzzzzzzzzzzzzzzzzzzzjjjjjjjjjjjjjjjjjjjjjjjjjjjjsssssssssssss ssssssffffffffffffffffffffffffffzzzzzzzzzzzzzzzzzzxxxxxxxxxxxxxxxxxjjj jjjjjjjjjjjjjjjjjjjjjjjjkkkkkkkkkkkkkkkkkkkkkkkzzzzzzzzzzzzzzckckck ckck...............zzzzzzzzzzz...............ckckckckckzzzzzzzzzzz

zzzxxxx................xxxxxxxxxxxxxxxxxxxxxxxkkkkkkkkkkkkkkk
kkkzzzzzzzzzzzzjjjjjjjjjjkkkkkkkkkkkkkkxxxxxxxxxxxxxxx.........xxxx
xxxxxxxxxzzzzzzzzzzzzzzbbbbbbbbbbbbbbbbbbbbbbvvvvvvvvvvvvv
vvvkkkkkkkkkkkkkkkkkttttXxxxxxxxxkkkkkkkkkkkkzzzzzzzzzz......
....zzzzzzzzzzchchchchchjjjjjjjjjjjjkkkkkkkkzzzzzzzzzzzzzzzzzzzzzz
zchchchchchxxxxxxxxxxxxzzzzzz.........zzzzzzzzzzzzzzzzzzzzzjjjjj
jjjjjjjjjjjjjjjjjjjjjjjsssssssssssssssssssssffffffffffffffffffffffffffzzzzzzzzzzzzzzz
zzzzxxxxxxxxxxxxxxxxxjjjjjjjjjjjjjjjjjjjjjjjjjjjjjjjjkkkkkkkkkkkkkkkkkk
kkkkkzzzzzzzzzzzzzzckckckckck................zzzzzzzzzzz............
...ckckckckckzzzzzzzzzzzzzzzzxxxx................xxxxxxxxxxxxxxx
xxxxxxkkkkkkkkkkkkkkkkkkkkzzzzzzzzzzzjjjjjjjjjjkkkkkkkkkkkkkkkxx
xxxxxxxxxxxx........

    "Mr David....!" A carer was gently shaking his shoulder,
"Would you like a cup of tea? A cup of tea and some cake....?
    xxxxxxxssssssssssssssskkkkkkkkkkkkkkkkfffffffffffffffffxxxx
zzzzzzzzzzzzzzzzzzzzzjjjjjjjjjjjjjjjjjjjjjjjjjjjjjjsssssssssssssssssssffffffffff
ffffffffffffffffzzzzzzzzzzzzzzzzzzzxxxxxxxxxxxxxxxxxjjjjjjjjjjjjjjjjjjjjjj
jjjjjjkkkkkkkkkkkkkkkkkkkkkkkkkkzzzzzzzzzzzzzckckckckck.........
.......zzzzzzzzzzz...............ckckckckckzzzzzzzzzzzzzzzzxxxx
xxxxxxxxxxxxxxxzzzzzzzzzzzzzzbbbbbbbbbbbbbbbbbbbbbvvvvvvvvvv
vvvvvvvkkkkkkkkkkkkkkkkttttttttttttttttttfffffffffffffffxxxxxxxxxxxxxxx
xxzzzzzzzzzzzzzzzzzzzzzzjjjjjjjjjjjjjjjjjjjjzzzzzzzzzzzzzzzzzzzzkkkkkkkk
kkkkkkkkktttttttttttttfffffffffffffxxxxxxxxxxxxxxxxxxxxzzzzzzzzzzzzzzzz
zzzzzjjjjjjjjjjjjjjjjjjjjzzzzzzzzzzzzzzzzzzzzkkkkkkkkkkkkkkkkkk...

    "David! It's time for your tablets! Take this please! And a drink
of water please, that's right ...."
    xxxxkkkkkxxxxxxxxxxxxxxxwater...zzzzzzzzzzzzzzxxxxxxxxx
xxkkkkkkkkkkkkkkkkjjjjjjjjjjjjjjjjjjjjjjjzzzzzzzzzzzzzzzzzzxxxxxxxxx
xxkkkkkkkkkkkkkkkkkkkkkkkkkkzzzzzzzzzzzzzzzzzzzzxxxxxxxxxxx
xxxkkkkkkkkkkkkkkkjjjjjjjjjjjjjjjjjjjjjkkkkkkkkkkkkkkkkkkkkkkxxxxxx
xxxxxxxxxzzzzzzzzzzzzzzzzzzzjjjjjjjjjjjjjzzzzzzzzzzzzzzzzzzzzxxxxxxxxx
xx

    "David! Hi there! It's me, Sarah." His reaction was slow. I had
planned four days for him back at the house, a summer break. I
arrived to find him unprepared and sunk in......what state of mind?
ffzzzzzzzzzzzzzzzzzzzzzzjjjjjjjjjjjjjjjjjjjjjjjjjjjjjsssssssssssssssssssffffffff
ffffffffffffffffffzzzzzzzzzzzzzzzzzzxxxxxxxxxxxxxxxxxjjjjjjjjjjjjjjjjjjjj
jjjjjjjkkkkkkkkkkkkkkkkkkkkkkkzzzzzzzzzzzzckckckckck.........
.......zzzzzzzzzzz...............ckckckckckzzzzzzzzzzzzzzzzxxxx...

.............xxxxxxxxxxxxxxxxxxxxxxxxkkkkkkkkkkkkkkkkkkzzzzzzz
zzzzjjjjjjjjjkkkkkkkkkkkkkkxxxxxxxxxxxxxxx

I   had   to   wait   for   him   to   surface.
..............kkkkkkxxxxxxxxffffffbbxxxxxxxxxxxxxxxxxxxxxxzzzzzzz
zzzzzzzzkkkkkkkkffffx

xxxxkkkkkkxxxxxxxxxxxxxxx......zzzzzzzzzzzzzzzxxxxxxxxxxxxkkk
kkkkkkkkkkkkjjjjjjjjjjjjjjjjjjjjjjjjjzzzzzzzzzzzzzzzzzzzxxxxxxxxxxxxkkk
kkkkkkkkkkkkkkkkkkkkkkzzz "

David, it's me!"

He was reacting now, to my voice.

"Did I surprise you?"

David's head lifted; a smile, a small smile, came over his face.

I sat; held his hand, leaned in to him.

His voice was low, difficult to vocalise. "I wan...."

"Say it again. I didn't catch what you said."

He tried again..."I want to..."

"Once again...You want to...?"

"Want to..." he repeated low, "to... to bind you to my soul!"

My eyes filled with tears, "Oh sweetheart...! Come on; we're going back to the house. I'm taking you back to the house for the weekend....Don't you remember?"

Another smile, steadier now.

"Are you ready? Let's go."

A ROOM FULL OF BOOKS

Diyarbakr (*Turkey*)
diyarbakr was old
when the romans were new
in this treacleblack stone, this slow
basaltic sludge stared at
by poppies
exfoliating in
40 degrees Celsius

scorpion old

& in the hills the heroes,
on their backs too
a swollen sting,
dosed up with heroin they
grimace as they bite
into green
exploding peppers

dreaming the university of night

raki clouding at twatlight
the cockstrut of soldiers
holding hands, sniffing roses,
about them the cells
of goldsmiths, silver shapers
tinbeaters, flyswarming meatsellers
cobblers gobbling nails

all this old as Tamberlaine

& now the neon windows
the orange
negligées, the pavilions of Paris
the petals opened for you
the desperation
like heads in a plastic bag
hearts like birds searching for windows

old as the conquest of someone else's woman.

October 2007

At home and in the car, the radio was playing a lot of the time and in its regular bulletins Turkey was in the news with Kurdish militants attacking Turkish patrols from hidden bases across the Iraqi border. David had spent his first two years as a teacher in Eastern Turkey. David and Colin together, with copies of Robert Graves, Yeats and the "Alexandrian Quartet" in their suitcases, had set off to experience the world and plunder it for poetry.

Now, as I leafed through the newspaper looking for items of news which might catch his attention, I wondered if David would be interested to know what was happening.

"The Kurds are having another go at getting their own government." "It says here," I read out, "'PKK attack on Turkish military. Turkish government threatens action on bases in Northern Iraq.'"

David nodded impassively.

"Diyarbakr, that's where you were, wasn't it?"

He looked me in the eyes this time, over the top of his glasses. I noticed how his eyes had changed in recent years, but couldn't describe to myself just how. The blue perhaps a little lighter? Ever so slightly watery? Slow-moving, less alert and focussed than before? If I were to suppose that the eyes are windows to the soul, I was fearful to look too long and deeply into his. They still held power and when David had something urgent to say – while his voice was weak – the eyes commanded attention.

"Eastern Turkey…."

"Can you remember where you lived? Did you and Colin share a house?"

He nodded vaguely; not a lot to add. If I wanted to know more I would have to ask Colin.

"Let me read you the poem," I suggested. David nodded happily and smiled at the images as I read.

"It's good!" I commented and David nodded emphatically. "I like the cobblers gobbling nails: tell me about them!" and David demonstrated: a mouth full of nails and hammering them into imaginary shoes.

"But not the last line: too much machismo! What do you think?"

A wry smile, not conceding the point.

There was a disturbance; I looked to see who was coming into the room. It was one of the residents, Helen, a kindly lady who in her vagueness nonetheless radiated cheerfulness. I had got to know Helen and noticed that she was always neatly dressed, 1950s style, with ankle socks and sensible shoes, a cardigan usually worn over a viyella blouse. I reckoned she must be about sixty, but with a youthful demeanour, a voice which reminded you of a benevolent school prefect somewhere between plumminess and the lacrosse pitch. Her easy smile and lively blue eyes seemed to look hopefully for signs of fun or entertainment. Today she carried a duster.

"Hello dear, so nice of you to be here," she acknowledged me benevolently. "Do excuse me interrupting; I just have to...." She waved her duster vaguely in our direction.

I smiled and left her to carry on.

Helen advanced to the bookshelf examining the photographs in their frames, of David and the boys, another of David and his brother. Apparently the photos were in need of dusting; at any rate she took them, one by one, giving them a good clean then arranged and re-arranged them.

I watched her doing the dusting with a demeanour that was wistfully cheerful, and couldn't help wondering just who it was that I was looking at: perhaps the shadow of Helen's old self? I tried to imagine her ten or twenty years ago. I saw a person who was helpful, understanding, never imposing herself, co-operative and persuasive.

David was unperturbed by the activity going on around him and was dozing off in his chair. I sat quietly, letting Helen get on with the job.

She chatted away as she worked, dusting the photographs, commenting and explaining.

"They're my brothers. ... There they are, that's better, and this one is my son.... So sorry to disturb you dears.... I do admire the way you... I always think it's frightfully important to... don't you think? Now if we all make an effort... I can see that you have a lot on your mind dear... I always say that once we get going we can... Thank you. No, don't let me disturb you.... Oh dear, I'll have to mend these socks.... I expect it will be time to...."

Holding David's hand as he dozed in his chair, I imagine Helen as she had been. I note fragments of speech, colloquialisms from a particular date and setting, the selection of familiar phrases strung together, remnants of a style forming what was now just the outline of a script. In Helen's script there was no trace of argumentativeness or aggression. As I listened I could identify only the repertoire of a person who had organised and run things, had been there to lend a helping hand, had chivvied people a little and looked after them a lot, laughed with them and loved being part of a family.

The style was still there although the content was missing, and I could see this person so clearly.

Helen finished her dusting and her rearranging. With one photograph clasped in her hand she lay down on David's bed and dozed off.

After a few moments a carer looked in and, seeing Helen lying there, looked enquiringly at me.

"Don't worry. It's quite alright. She was just dusting the pictures."

"She misses her family so much," the carer told me. "It's nearly supper time," she added. "Will you help David? I'll give Helen a hand."

I walked David along the wide, carpeted corridor. Holding my arm, he supported himself on the other side by the bar, set at waist-height along the wall.

As we made our way to supper I paused looking at the pictures on the walls: repro photos of people and times supposed to ring a bell, chime a chord. This was one of the best care homes in the county – probably the best – and this floor, where David and others with similar problems were cared for, had been named "Memory Lane". I found it rather cloying, but told myself I shouldn't judge by my own impatient standards. The pictures and photos catered for different interests: here for instance were two glamorous poster-style photographs, both in full colour, of Marylyn Monroe and Audrey Hepburn. On the other side the illustrations were definitely for a masculine taste: a stylised Harley Davidson motorcycle, all black curves and gleaming chrome, several World War One planes and an army truck from the same era. Further along the corridor, framed reproductions of old railway posters advertised the Cornish Riviera, Nice and St Tropez.

"I like them," I thought, "They're cheerful and colourful – things that we can all enjoy".

Supper was taken in the homely space of a kitchen diner, where the carers served up the food, brought from the kitchens below and kept warm. Getting everyone settled took time. When I arrived with David, several were seated already but harmony was not prevailing. One gentleman had used his elbow to express aggression towards a woman.

"Stupid cow! What's the point of...," followed by expletives and a swipe with the walking-stick.

A carer ran to calm the man, took the stick and soothed the victim.

To me the small incident was shocking; I looked at David to see how he reacted; there was a mild expression on his face and nothing more – any hint of a reaction? I could not be sure and could not know whether he registered such incidents, or viewed them as just natural.

Perhaps the shocked reaction existed in my mind only but it was clear to me that, while David had become warmer and more gentle as the affliction progressed, the route for others was in the direction of aggression, verbal venom and physical violence.

David was seated at a table now and soup was on the menu. Carers helped those who could not feed themselves, or would not.

I kissed him and made my way out, hoping that he would be busy eating and not feeling sad; it was hard to read his mind –

perhaps here too the sadness was more in my mind than in his? I couldn't know.

Once in the car and round the first few bends in the road, to switch my mind I turned on the radio. A year ago I had driven this first half mile blinded by tears: now I could accept that David was alright: that my sadness lasted longer than his and that my guilt was beginning to recede. If I wanted to know about David, the place to look now was his study and the shelves of papers and books. On the radio it was the six o'clock news: Turkey again and its struggle with the Kurds. To David now this was just so much noise.

A WELSH HILLSIDE

Death
The fool lay giggling at some distance from
his severed goggling head. Death was still
creaking as he scythed. There were
hands, half-clenched, everywhere, huge thumb
and talon fingers, aware that to tear
the gauze of matter from the soul
will let it swirl into another form

As cloud above the clay he gazed
in greed at the bright alphabet of night
knowing god was the endless
interchange of signs, white's blaze
on black, each atom's game of chess,
each beach's breaking wave. The wise were right
to grace this interlude with praise.

Spinning now he is shown all history
revolving through the multitudes
asking why the gods who chariot space
should store their spirit in the tree
of man. The next birth his turning face
will grin again and grow to see the fish
gasping for the waterbearer's version of the mystery

February 2008
Although I had been writing about David as the illness developed, when he died the shock was just too great and there was no thought of doing any more. Joe and Nigel were deeply affected and grieved with me, not just for the person we had lost but also for the person we had begun to lose so many years ago. The staff of the nursing home were equally shocked since the pneumonia which had eventually caused David's death crept up so quickly and unexpectedly. Remarkably, it was by them that his qualities of warmth and humour, welling up through his impairments, had been most appreciated and they grieved for his parting.

Joe and Nigel shared with me the burden of the administrative details which had to be seen to. Like most families I suspect, our over-riding priority was to arrange a funeral service that would express all we wanted to say. A church service was perhaps not what we wanted, given that David's views on religion were not at all conventional; nonetheless we were persuaded by an understanding and sensitive vicar, – even though he hadn't known David – that a service of thanksgiving in the village church would provide the best opportunity to pay all those tributes. And it was the right decision. We included a reading from the Wisdom of Solomon, a hymn that had been sung at our wedding, and a tribute from Colin, his best friend, which recalled David's glory days. Colin spoke of their early travels together in Turkey and Ethiopia, of David's work with the Organisation and his commitment to poetry. Joe and Nigel spoke their own moving tributes with memories of growing up in Muscat with their father. The only slightly discordant note came in the vicar's address when he assured us that, despite his unbelief David would be joyfully received in heaven. Had I really told him that David did not believe in God? Perhaps by mentioning David's misgivings about the Church I had indeed given that impression but I didn't think I had ever said he was an out and out atheist. It was, typically, a question to which David had never given me a straight answer. Perhaps David thought that, as far as the idea of God was concerned, some people had got the wrong end of the stick or were looking at the question the wrong way round.

That awkward moment in the sermon passed quickly however and the service was inspiring and not at all conventional. "Across The Universe" started it, one of David's favourite Beatles tracks and at the conclusion, "Golden Slumber" and "Carry That Weight" right through to "The End", the final track. It made a remarkably poignant finale and Joe remarked that he would never be able to listen to those tracks again without remembering the moment.

After the service friends back at the house greeted us.

"You really did him justice," Colin told us. "It was a good show." In a way I felt that was the right word and that David would have approved of it, a show in his honour, tightly packed with details carefully selected to pay him tribute and to show how we felt about him.

Joe and Nigel went off to talk to their own friends who had come along. My neighbour, Pam, came up to me.

"I never knew he had such an adventurous life!"

"That's because you only knew him for the last ten years," I replied. "He packed a lot into the earlier years!"

"Well, it was fascinating to hear all about your life together and all the rest of it."

I was gratified; that was exactly what I had hoped.

"There are so many friends and neighbours like you who never knew anything about his early days, when he was such a dynamic and energetic person," I told her. "One thing about David was that he wasn't afraid to take risks." I took pride in saying this. "He would take on new ideas and follow them up, straight away, with action." Pam nodded, eager to know more.

"In his personal life it didn't always work out too well," I added ruefully. "But in his work with the Organisation it was a great strength."

Two colleagues from the old days with the Organisation nodded agreement.

"He was also the best boss I ever had; more of a mentor than a line-manager."

"He was generous with his time and wise in his advice," another added.

These were the sentiments which act like healing warmth to hurting spirits. Thanks to the thoughtfulness and comfort of friends, we were able to remember all the brilliant things about David, which had somehow become less real as his abilities declined, and we could tell those friends who had only known him in the recent years about David in his best days.

In the quiet, low, days following the funeral, the thinking started up. I found myself with an intractable circle that I could not square: how to reconcile the fact that now as I delved through his poems and his library of books, and as I went on to retrace some of his early years, in many respects I was beginning to know David so much better. It seemed as if, in many ways, he was now much more with me; and yet, to my despair, he was not there. I started up long conversations in my head that I wished we had had. I saw how I could hold an opinion and argue it with him; take a stand and gain a point of view from time to time, which could have made our relationship easier and the role reversal, when it came, less painful.

June 2008

I chose the summer solstice to return with Joe and Nigel to the Welsh mountain village where David was born and grew up, to scatter his ashes on the hillside. The midsummer date seemed a good time to choose and I felt sure David would have approved. Afterwards we visited the sites of his poems – the little church with its devil's door, the pump, now just a piece of village memorabilia but in David's young day the source of water for the village, the pub where "the skies began babbling in Welsh". We visited the primary school, used now as the village hall but still displaying the honours board with David's name in gold letters, awarded a scholarship to Grammar School at the age of nine – we had always been impressed by that. Then we visited the grammar school which he had travelled to by bus from the cross-roads below the village.

There were still a few relatives living in the village and at the end of the day we were invited for tea. I could not help wondering why David had not brought us here more frequently. Did he find it difficult to relate to a family that he had moved away from? Because his parents had both died so early in his life, did the village hold painful memories? Yet his poems painted the village in lively detail. Its memories were obviously close and clear.

The relatives welcomed us with tea and cakes and brought out black and white photographs of David, wearing a school blazer and a 1960's haircut. My sons studied these with interest and their new-found elderly cousin studied the two young men in her turn.

"The likeness is there – can't you see it? I know the hair-cuts are different!"

"It's a pity Mostyn isn't here," her sister added. "He was at school with David, and they lived opposite each other," she explained to me.

We drank our tea and finished our cake before taking leave and returning to the lane for a final walk in the gentle Welsh air. I would have liked to talk with Mostyn. If he and David had grown up together, Mostyn must have a lot of memories of the two of them and I regretted that we had missed him. But in this I was mistaken for, as we walked down the lane, someone was coming up the hill towards us and as we exchanged walkers' greetings something prompted me to ask.

"Are you by any chance Mostyn?"

Yes, it was Mostyn, and he was happy to share memories.

"David was in a different league from me," he told us. "He went away and..." Mostyn waved his arms vaguely. "He went away and... did a lot of things. I've stayed here all my life, in the village!"

If I had been more polite I would have asked for more about himself: did he regret not going away? How had his life been in the village? But I only wanted to hear what he had to say about David. I nodded, hoping for more.

"He was different from his brothers and sisters. I think... you know..."

He paused, searching for words and I waited. Standing there in the lane in the damp air it seemed for a moment as if I was hoping for some revelation.

But there was no revelation. After a thoughtful pause Mostyn said quite simply, "I think, you know, David had a different way of looking at things, different from the rest of his family..."

That was all, but I recognised it as the same recurring theme: David saw things differently, differently as far as I was concerned, from anyone else I knew. It was of course, was what had attracted me to him, thirty years ago.

I had written my chronicle partly to give vent to feelings of helplessness and partly to recall the time before the illness started, David's "glory days", but also because, in the isolation of my position – which, of course, I recognise was by no means unique – I felt strongly that others should have a chance to listen and hear what I had to say. Spending the day in the scenes of David's Welsh childhood, with Snowdon on the horizon catching the intermittent sun, reminded me of what I had stated at the outset: that I was writing in order to understand. But what was it that had to be understood? Was it the meaning of David's life and of our lives together? Perhaps it was also to find an answer to the conundrum that David had posed – love or adventure? And whether the two were mutually exclusive.

STARDUST

The Tower
Those who stay inside the tower
bluffing out the dragon's breath
forget the sun's a blaze of souls.
They revolve inside the hour
stasis stasis in their bowels
in their skulls the spoon of death
lobotomising dreams of power

Those who on the turrets stand
gazing on the dragon's scales
noting liquid plays of light
will not fall upon the land
when the bolting thunder strikes.
They will hoist their leprous scales
and drown where drowning's planned.

Those whose towers are the locked
molecules of frozen light
where the stone is latticework
see when sun is thundershocked
watch the dragons in the murk
fetch the starchild from the night
write the last word in their book.

In the year following David's death I immersed myself in his books. They were in a jumbled state and simply putting them in order was an absorbing task and satisfactorily time-consuming. The largest section was poetry along with biographies and books about the poets. Next in number were books on symbolism, myths and fantasy: I grouped these in an order that I chose, starting with the most esoteric, books on tarot and Egyptian mysteries, and at the other end Arthurian and Welsh tales up to the fantasy novels of Philip Pullman and Terry Pratchett. It took some time as I frequently stopped to discover something new or reread a favourite story. When that section was in some sort of order I moved on to

David's collection of linguistics texts which I arranged next to works on semiotics and cultural studies by Raymond Williams, John Berger and Linda Colley. David had also a fair number of volumes on philosophy, psychology and anthropology which had been the subject of his first degree. The sorting and sifting was taking me weeks, really because I was constantly being drawn in to the various subject matters, as if I were following David down the various roads of his reading, finding new insights into the development of his thinking and the ideas behind his poetry. Wasn't this all familiar ground already? Well, only in a very limited way. When you are busy doing other things – which in my case included, firstly, bringing up children and then, later, worrying about David's health – it doesn't leave much room for intellectual reflection in any depth. Now it was different, and I had time to explore where David had been.

One theme that cropped up as I was sorting and grouping the volumes into coherent subject headings, was the subject of metaphor and I decided those books formed a separate group on their own. Many of the volumes had notes in the margin and passages underlined and I felt that this topic had excited David more than many others. I thought that, if his illness had not intervened, this was the subject that David might have studied and written about seriously and in depth, the subject which perhaps would have tied together many of his other interests. I selected one volume to make a start on.

Alongside that I found myself, almost accidentally, reading books about science, of which there were a few in David's collection. At about that time a newspaper supplement about genetics and a book about Darwin – who had been one of David's heroes – inspired me to understand rather more about the life sciences than I had done. DNA and metaphor worked very well together, especially when Joe, visiting one day, dropped a book in my lap, which would have suited David down to the ground. It was a combination of Gaia theory and speculation of a cosmic and spiritual order on life and its origins.

"Dad would have loved this. It's right up his street," I told Joe.

"I know!" he smiled.

"But the tone of it is very – well, rhapsodic I think is how I would describe it."

"So? What's wrong with that?" Joe challenged.

"I like it! I like the theme of the book...very much. Especially the musings about where life begins, and the conscious universe. But what I think is," I hesitated, "I mean, I don't think that most scientists will buy into the rhapsodic, quite poetical language."

"I don't see why not!"

The fact that Joe was unconvinced surprised me. He had always shrugged off poetry and wanted to pin things down to the concrete and rational.

So I continued to read along the twin tracks; evolutionary life science and treatises on metaphor. One idea led on to another and, to my delight, in David's library there was nearly always a volume to answer my queries, either to take me further forward or else back to his poetry. At last the more enigmatic of his poems began to yield up secrets. And to my surprise I began to find clues to the nature of David's mystical thinking.

Through various serendipitous readings, I followed up these lines of thought. They included a series of weekend supplements, one on the origins of the universe, another on the role of stars in seeding the planet. *Wikipedia* helped to get my head around the science of cells and bacteria and the encoding of information by DNA. In this way I began to see the links in David's poems between such disparate and romantic ideas as star dust, the lost libraries of Alexandria, genetic information and the spiral shapes of fossils. I could begin to grasp how his poems explored these themes alongside the achievements of poets, philosophers and scientists. It felt as if I were cracking David's codes and understanding that metaphor and playfulness lay at the heart of them.

More than ever I wanted David to be there. Not David as he was in his last years but the one I first knew, so that I could hold a decent conversation. I would ask him if I had at last begun to understand his poems.

"*So is that what you were getting at when you wrote these lines?*" I imagined myself saying.

And he would surely reply, teasingly because he would never give a direct answer to a philosophical question. "*Perhaps. Something like that!*"

And I would ask him what he thought of some more recent themes and theories, the ones which, in recent years, his decaying intellect had been unable to grasp. And we would have a brilliant conversation.

"This week is a year since David left me. I heard him last night in an owl that hooted."

Grief takes many forms and it also comes back and seizes you unaware. I was sailing along at the time, quite calm, despite knowing that it was nearly a year, and then a sudden sleepless night took me unprepared. It must have been about four in the morning – very dark outside, and silent. The owl hooted and I heard it dimly through my state of not being quite asleep. Half awake and half asleep I heard the owl and found the thought in my head: "*Imagine it was David speaking. That would be just too fanciful, wouldn't it?*"

I had come awake by now and the simple act of imagining David in the hooting of an owl had made my eyes fill with tears. The night was very quiet again. How silly to let myself think those thoughts.

But the thoughts wouldn't go away of course and in the darkness I heard it – the owl – one more time. Shocked and disorientated I sat up.

Oh David! David! David! Is that you? I clutched my head and let the tears flow.

I felt him so close in the darkness: so close and so not there.

And I knew that outside there was only an owl.

What I really wanted was to carry on those conversations and of course I could do that, through David's books and the other sources they would lead to. I knew that, and I had said so a year ago. I was, however, surprised to find it had come true and to find I was making progress.

One day out of the blue Sugar phoned. Of course Sugar is not her real name and it took me a while to realise who this person with the slightly American accent was, and also how she had obtained my phone number. She wanted to know how David was. Felt it was time to, "catch up, for old times' sake".

I had to tell her and summarise in brief sentences the happenings of the last thirty years, but first I had to tell her, "David died last year."

She was silent, then, "I'm so sorry. What happened?"

I told her about the Parkinson's and the decline of his mind, but also about the comfortable surroundings and care of the last two years. The sudden end.

"I wish I had known. I would have come."

It was to me a relief that she had not known and that she had not come, either to visit or to the funeral. I didn't know how I would have coped with that and was glad I had been spared the test. In any case, David had moved on in many ways and, with the important exception of in his poetry, David had never been much inclined to revisit the past.

"And how are you?" I asked – politely, I hoped. "How is your life?"

"I went to America," she told me. "Ended up working in real estate. My husband is American. We're both about to retire; if we can. It's not a good time right now. What I was wondering was…."

I felt something unwelcome approaching

"I – we, were wondering about the… the pension thing…."

I tried to imagine what she had in mind. Perhaps it was whether, as a divorcee, she had any rights.

"You had better write to the Organisation," I suggested. "But I don't think there would be anything in it."

"Hmm."

I gave her the address. I also suggested she write to the government's Work and Pensions department to see if she was entitled to any state pension, although it seemed doubtful since she had left the country so long ago. I felt sure, that none of this was what she wanted to hear but she took it well and responded brightly.

"I'm sure we'll get by. We always do and life seems to turn out OK in the end. Nice to talk to you!"

"You too," I replied and added the usual signing-off formula. "Take care!"

I wish I could end this story by relating that I had, indeed, carried on David's work and had produced a paper which, with a fine synthesis of science and metaphor, expressed his ideas clearly, moving the debate around science and poetry, religion and society forward to a really significant extent. I wish too that I could say that Joe and Nigel, our two sons, had set up in partnership, working on the neuroscience of cognitive impairment and nearing a breakthrough which would bring untold benefits to those suffering from dementia. I wish I could say that my own business, which I had set up to improve the English of those foreign care-workers who staff our nursing homes and care for our near and dear ones, had succeeded in obtaining for them the recognition and appreciation of their employers and managers and the wider public.

I cannot say any of these things and can only say that some of them are pure fantasy and some of them are work in progress.

May 2009

A MISTED MIRROR: EARLY RESPONSES

"A moving and honest account of the impact of caring for someone with Parkinsons and Dementia. We recognize the impact of the gradual and ongoing daily losses over many years and the metamorphosis of Sarah from friend, lover, and wife to the main carer for her husband. This book will help anyone who is feeling guilty that they are not superhuman; not always the perfect loving carer that they would like to be."
—Joy Watkins, Development Lead Uniting Carers, Dementia UK, www.dementiauk.org

"*A Misted Mirror* is a haunting, harrowing and very bravely-written memoir, presented as fiction. Gillian Jones demonstrates the skilled craft of a novelist as she takes the reader through the complex problems involved in looking after a once brilliant man, her husband and a poet, who has Parkinson's disease. The vulnerability, trauma, and conflicting emotions she dares reveal will strike many a chord with every reader who has had to care for someone close to them. In the process of her memoir, she re-discovers the man she was married to in more depth and detail than in the years of their marriage. This is a human, heartfelt read, and an important book in its rawness and depth."
—Patricia McCarthy. Editor, Agenda Poetry, http://www.agendapoetry.co.uk

"This book is mainly about poetry, beautiful poetry that happens to have been written in the lifetime of a man who died of dementia. It has now been crafted into prose, as 'fiction based on fact', by his widow. Some eight years have passed since Keith Jones's poetry, like Plath's, helped me look after myself and some one else important to me and now, three years after his death, Gillian Jones's prose provides the setting that makes this poetry accessible to many."
—Dr Nick Clarke, Consultant in Old Age Psychiatry, MBBS, MRCPsych, MD.

"This book should be on every doctor's and nurse's reading list. It delivers an insight into the impact physical and mental disability has on family relationships. The fact that it is also entertaining and highly readable will make it a pleasurable 'must tell-my-friends-about-it' item on anyone's reading list."
—Dr Catherine Brogan, MBBS MSc FFPHM

NOTES

[1] Keith Jones wrote more than one version of this final line. In another version, the last word of 'The Emperor' is "Love".

[2] Quoted from Kathleen Raine, [no title], in Jane Williams (ed.), *Tambimuttu: Bridge Between Two Worlds*, London, Peter Owen, 1989, p. 69.

[3] Brian Patten, [no title], in, *Tambimuttu*, p. 181.

[4] Jean MacVean, "Tambi – A Personal View", in, *Tambimuttu*, p. 179.

[5] The same.

[6] The same.

[7] The same.

[8] The same.

[9] Quoted as it appears in, *Tambimuttu*, p. 107.

[10] Timothy Leary, "Tambimuttu Shines On", in *Tambimuttu*, p. 158.

[11] *Poetry London*, Issue no 1 (February 1939), as quoted by Geoffrey Elborn, "Remembering Tambimuttu", in *Tambimuttu*, p. 166.

[12] Robin Waterfield, "Introduction", in, *Tambimuttu*, p. 21.

[13] From the poem, 'Holly Bush Lane' (quoted at the beginning of Chapter 7.)

About Proverse Hong Kong

Proverse Hong Kong, co-founded by Gillian and Verner Bickley, is based in Hong Kong with strong regional and international connections.

Verner Bickley has led cultural and educational centres, departments, institutions and projects in many parts of the world. Gillian Bickley has recently concluded a career as a University teacher of English Literature spanning four continents. Proverse Hong Kong draws on their combined academic, administrative and teaching experience as well as varied long-term participation in reading, research, writing, editing, indexing, reviewing, publishing and authorship.

Proverse Hong Kong has published novels, novellas, non-fiction (including history, sport, travel), single-author poetry collections, young teens and academic books. Other interests include biography, memoirs and diaries, and academic works in the humanities, social sciences, cultural studies, linguistics and education. Some Proverse books have accompanying audio texts. Proverse works with texts by non-native-speaker writers of English as well as by native English-speaking writers.

Proverse welcomes authors who have a story to tell, a person they want to memorialize, a neglect they want to remedy, a record they want to correct, a strong interest that they want to share, information or perceptions they want to offer, skills they want to teach, and who consciously seek to make a contribution to society in an informative, interesting and well-written way.

The name, "Proverse", combines the words "prose" and "verse" and is pronounced accordingly.

THE PROVERSE PRIZE

The Proverse Prize, an annual international competition for an unpublished publishable book-length work of fiction, non-fiction, or poetry, was established in January 2008. It is open to all who are at least eighteen on the date they sign the entry form and without restriction of nationality, residence or citizenship.

Its objectives are: to encourage excellence and / or excellence and usefulness in publishable written work in the English Language, which can, in varying degrees, "delight and instruct". Entries are invited from anywhere in the world.

CO-FOUNDERS

Dr Verner Bickley, MBE and Dr Gillian Bickley.
To celebrate their lifelong love of words in any form, as readers, listeners, performers, teachers, academics, writers, editors, indexers and now publishers.

HONORARY ADVISORS (2009-)

Marion Bethel (poet, the Bahamas), David Crystal (linguist and lexicographer, United Kingdom), Björn Jernudd (linguist, Sweden), Larry Smith (cultural administrator, USA), Edwin Thumboo (poet and academic, Singapore), Olga Walló (novelist, translator, Czech Republic).

HONORARY LEGAL ADVISOR: Mr Raymond T. L. Tse.
HONORARY JUDGES: Anonymous.
HONORARY UK AGENT AND DISTRIBUTOR: Miss Christine Penney
HONORARY ADMINISTRATORS: Proverse Hong Kong

Proverse Prize Winners / Joint-Winners

2009: Laura Solomon (New Zealand), Rebecca Jane Tomasis (Hong Kong).
2010: Gregory James (Hong Kong and UK), Gillian Jones (UK).
2011: Announcement of the finalists, 22 November 2011.

A Misted Mirror

Summary Terms and Conditions (*for indication only & subject to revision*)
The information below is for guidance only. Please refer to the year-specific Proverse Prize Entry Form & Terms & Conditions, which are uploaded, no later than 30 April each year, onto the Proverse Hong Kong website: <http://www.proversepublishing.com>. To receive current information, email <info@proversepublishing.com> to be put on the free Proverse e-Newsletter mailing-list. Between 1 February and 1 May annually, you may request a copy of the details and entry form, by writing to: "The Proverse Prize, Proverse Hong Kong, P.O. Box 259, Tung Chung Post Office, Tung Chung, Lantau Island, NT, Hong Kong, SAR, China", enclosing a large (A4 OR A5 size) self-addressed envelope. For enquiries from Hong Kong, please affix a HKD4.40 postage stamp. For international entries, please enclose seven IRC coupons.

The Prize
1) Publication by Proverse Hong Kong, with
2) Cash prize of HKD10,000 (HKD7.80 = approx. US$1.00)
Supplementary editing / publication grants may be made to selected other entrants for publication by Proverse Hong Kong.
Depending on the quality of the work in any year, the prize may be shared by at most two entrants or withheld, as recommended by the judges.
The entry fee is HKD200 OR GBP30.
Writers are eligible, who are at least eighteen on the date they sign their entry form(s) for The Proverse Prize. There is no nationality or residence restriction.

Each submitted work must be an unpublished publishable single-author work of non-fiction, fiction or poetry, the original work of the entrant, and submitted in the English language. Plays and school textbooks are ineligible.

Translated work: If the work entered is a translation from a language other than English, both the original work and the translation should be previously unpublished. This is not a translation prize. The submitted work will not be judged as a translation but as an original work.

Extent of the Manuscript: within the range of what is usual for the genre of the work submitted. However, it is advisable that novellas be in the range 35,000 to 50,000 words); other fiction (e.g. novels, short-story collections) and non-fiction (e.g. autobiographies, biographies, diaries, letters, memoirs, essay collections, etc.) should be in the range, 80,000 to 110,000 words. Poetry collections should be in the range, 8,000 to 30,000 words. Other word-counts and mixed-genre submissions are not ruled out.

Writers may choose, if they wish, to obtain the services of an Editor in presenting their work, and should acknowledge this help and the nature and extent of this help in the Entry Form.

KEY DATES FOR THE AWARD OF THE PROVERSE PRIZE IN ANY YEAR (subject to confirmation and/or change*)

Deadline for receipt of Entry Fees/ Entry Forms	31 May of the year of entry
Deadline for receipt of entered manuscripts	30 June of the year of entry
Announcement of long-list	August-September of the year of entry*
Announcement of short-list	October-December of the year of entry*
Announcement of winner/ max two winners (sharing the cash prize)	December of the year of entry to April of the year that follows the year of entry*
Cash Award Made	After November of the year that follows the year of entry*
Publication of winning work(s)	After November of the year that follows the year of entry (e.g. for entries in May/June 2011, after November 2012 onwards)*

A Misted Mirror

Books published by, or available through, Proverse Hong Kong
http://www.proversepublishing.com

*Indicates a title is already available from our Hong Kong based Distributor,
The Chinese University Press of Hong Kong, The Chinese University of Hong Kong, Shatin, NT,
Hong Kong, SAR, China. Email: cup@cuhk.edu.hk

HONG KONG WORLD BOOKS

FICTION

CEMETERY – MISS YOU by Jason S Polley. Hong Kong and the UK, November 2011. Preface by Ina Grigorova. pbk. 144pp. ISBN: 978-988-19932-8-1.

"The story of this man made me realize with chilled bones that there are places on earth where the known laws of social physics simply fall apart. ... The people and events in the story are grainy, pixelated, blinking on and off; reality has been exposed at the Planck scale where any apparent continuity breaks down. // Hong Kong is a good substrate for Sci-Fi constructs, not just because Hong Kong is so insanely futuristic, a spread-out tower of Babel, and not just because if you squint you can picture *cemetery*'s characters crossing states more exotic than national boundaries (while borrowing each other's passports and pasts), but also because the book's very surface approaches quantum foam: objects of characterization blinking on and off, end-positioned subjects slipping away into the next sentence predicate; cause and effect inverting, like the thought-wave must flow in Saa Ji's native-tongue state... A text with the wheels of its own cognitive process both at work and exposed." – Ina Grigorova (from her Preface to *cemetery miss you*)

DEATH HAS A THOUSAND DOORS by Patricia Grey. Hong Kong and the UK, November 2011. pbk. 320pp. Proverse Prize Finalist 2010. ISBN-13: 978-988-19932-6-7.

Family complications abound in this mystery set in the little-known Pyrenean country of Andorra. "We travel through the mountains, villages and history of Andorra, through the histories and stories of its characters, as a family comes together to search for its missing sister and daughter. – An irresistible suspenseful read from start to finish." – Rebecca Tomasis, author of *Mishpacha – Family* (Proverse Prize Joint-Winner 2009)
"The works of English speakers who came to visit Andorra in the last two centuries are an essential part of our literary heritage. Patricia Grey's book is a step forward, a new milestone. From the premises of contemporary fiction she offers us a new perspective of our little world, so close, so complex, so unknown."— Albert Villaró, Andorran writer, author of *Blau de Prússia* (Carlemany prize 2006)

HILARY AND DAVID by Laura Solomon. Hong Kong and the UK, November 2011. pbk. 184pp. Proverse Prize Publication Prize 2010. ISBN: 978-988-19932-9-8.

Although they are on opposite sides of the world, email friends Hilary in New Zealand and David in London share their thoughts on life, the universe, men, women and everything else in between and provide companionship and advice for one another.

"Absolutely unputdownable. Once you commence reading this England-New Zealand based novel you will find yourself carried on quickly via the impelling momentum generated by all the relationship and emotional hassles the two main characters have in their distinct yet interwoven lives on two sides of the World. Well-written. Interesting. Clever. Well done, Laura Solomon!" —Vaughan Rapatahana, author of the poetry collection,
Home, Away, Elsewhere (2011)
"I found myself caught up in the story and read the book in one sitting."
— Member, International Proverse Prize 2010 Judging Panel

*INSTANT MESSAGES by Laura Solomon. Hong Kong and the UK, 23 November 2010. pbk. 168pp. Proverse Prize Joint-Winner 2009. ISBN 978-988-19320-2-0.

A Misted Mirror

www.chineseupress.com/asp/e_Book_card.asp?BookID=2910&Lang=E

Life is tough for fifteen-year-old computer nerd Olivia Best. Her twin sister Melanie, who used to be Olivia's best friend, has taken to drinking and self-harming. Her father has no job and a string of unpublished romance novels to his name. Olivia's mother has just left Olivia's father for her lesbian yoga teacher, Sue. To top things off, Olivia is being severely bullied by a gang of boys from a neighbouring estate. Together with her trusted ally, a stuffed toy green frog, Olivia attempts to navigate the stormy seas of her existence.

"Hilarious!" "Excellent!" "Its light and ironic touch

JOCKEY, by Gillian Bickley (when Gillian Workman). Hong Kong, 1979. pbk. 64pp. (inc. several original illustrations and facsimilies). Written for young readers. Based on extensive research. Authentic background to the RHKJC. Suitable as a reference for adults interested in the history of the then Royal Hong Kong Jockey Club. Original illustrations. ISBN-10: 962-85570-3-3; ISBN-13: 978-962-85570-3-5.

*MISHPACHA – FAMILY by Rebecca Tomasis. Hong Kong and the UK, 23 November 2010. pbk. 316pp. inc. Glossary, Author portrait. Proverse Prize Joint-Winner (2009). Supported by the Hong Kong Arts Development Council. ISBN 978-988-19320-1-3.
http://www.chineseupress.com/asp/e_Book_card.asp?BookID=2911&Lang=E

"Passionate. A saga of women seeking identity." – Proverse Prize Judges.
"Outstanding … I was engrossed. In … [one] sense the novel deals with a universal issue – the dynamic relationships – between family and state, between cultures, between the varied world-views and motivations possessed by young and old generations. … *Mishpacha* touches me deeply. It is delightful to see that Hong Kong – an international city upholding freedom of creativity – has eventually became the birthplace of Mishpacha." – Yeeshan Yang, author of *Whispers* and *Moans* and *Palma's Tears*.

*THE MONKEY IN ME: CONFUSION, LOVE AND HOPE UNDER A CHINESE SKY by Caleb Kavon. Hong Kong and the UK, March 2009. pbk. 176pp. ISBN 978-988-17724-4-2.
www.chineseupress.com/asp/e_Book_card.asp?BookID=2521&Lang=E
Mobibook e-book edition (2009). ISBN-13: 978-988-17724-6-6.
www.mobipocket.com/en/eBooks/BookDetails.asp?BookID=150203&Origine=1042
24Reader Ebook edition (2010) ISBN 978-988-18479-6-6

"A dynamic exploration of human conscience in today's modern and economically aware Hong Kong. As the recession looms and new cultural trends develop, the book looks forward to the personal and societal changes that must be made. This witty, intelligent and insightful novel works as both an interesting read and a personal quest to find answers." – Stephanie Gaynor, *HK Magazine*, 13 March 2009.
"The main message Kavon communicates is that we live in a desert of low culture and tragic materialism. Humanity is doomed, and our retribution is here in the graceless fall of capitalism. His ode to Hong Kong, in a chapter entitled 'Place of Salvation', is sweet." – Anthony Carlyle, *Time Out*, 27 March 2009.

*A PAINTED MOMENT, by Jennifer Ching. Hong Kong and the UK, March 2010. pbk. 160pp. w. author's portrait (4C). Supported by the Hong Kong Arts Development Council. ISBN: 978-988-18905-1-1.
www.chineseupress.com/asp/e_Book_card.asp?BookID=2739&lang=E
Mobipocket Ebook edition (2010) ISBN 978-988-18905-6-6.

"In the work of Jennifer Ching, Hong Kong has found a new and welcome voice in fiction. And, as one among the many worlds well-chosen words create, *A Painted Moment* is a slender, but significant, novel. In it, the sum total of human experience pushes forward a fraction, inclining immeasurably (if perceptibly) towards the light. There is growth, there is being, there will be a

tomorrow. I look forward to Ms Ching's next novel unreservedly." – Stuart Christie.
"The main themes of the novel are self-growth and friendship. Ching has painstakingly illustrated the inevitable moment of self-independence pressing upon us in due time." – Flora Mak, in *Cha: An Asian literary Journal*, Issue 12, September 2010.

*THE RELUCTANT TERRORIST: IN THE PATH OF THE JIZO, by Caleb Kavon. Hong Kong, 2011. pbk. ISBN 978-988-19320-8-2.
http://www.chineseupress.com/asp/e_Book_card.asp?BookID=3050&Lang=E

In this novel, set in contemporary Hong Kong and Japan, with flashbacks to the Second World War, a Japanese businessman takes a deliberately modest revenge against another Japanese family that damaged his own during the Second World War. His surprising act of terrorism is a paradoxical gesture for peace. We meet again characters from Kavon's first novel, "The Monkey in me: Confusion, Love and Hope under a Chinese Sky" (2009).

REVENGE FROM BEYOND by Dennis Wong. Hong Kong and the UK, November 2011.
Preface by H. H. Judge Garry Tallentire, The District Court, Hong Kong. pbk. c. 176pp. b/w ills by the Author. Proverse Prize Publication Prize 2010. ISBN 13: 978-988-19932-5-0.

"Revenge From Beyond" is a wonderful insight into the role of the Judge/Magistrate in Imperial China. Set in the Tang Dynasty it portrays a judicial system of some sophistication yet steeped in brutality and unchallengeable power. ... A well-crafted satisfying read that both entertains and provides a vivid insight into the Judicial system of China in the Tang Dynasty. It is my profound hope that this is not the last we will hear of Judge Quan and I look forward to further adventures." – H.H. Judge Garry Tallentire, The District Court, Hong Kong.

*TIGHTROPE! – A BOHEMIAN TALE by Olga Walló. Hong Kong and the UK, November, 2010. Translated from Czech by Johanna Pokorny, Veronika Revická, & Others. Edited by Gillian Bickley & Olga Walló, with Verner Bickley. Poetry Translated by Justin Quinn, Veronika Revická. pbk. 272pp. 3 x 4C original illustrations by Monika Abbott.
ISBN 13: 978-988-18905-0-4.
www.chineseupress.com/asp/e_Book_card.asp?BookID=2942&Lang=E

An extraordinary, curiously intellectual small girl undertakes the demanding and costly burden of comprehending the world. Her father – a peculiar leftist intellectual, and her mother, a neurotic actress, belonging to an old farming family – are more or less social outcasts, who fight for survival. The situation prevailing in Socialist Eastern Europe in the period after the Second World War – which is both the setting and an inherent part of the fabric of this tale – produces incidents which are funny, cruel, and absurd, eliciting both laughter and compassion. The language of the Czech original is complicated and multileveled, intermixing rural dialect with communist Newspeak, theatre jargon with the lowest "proletarian" argot; and is lifted by the language of philosophical reflections and poetical associations. This English translation of the second volume of Olga Walló's admired novel trilogy based on her own life and times (*Spires of the Holy Spirit*) will certainly attract international readers and increase knowledge of Czech history and culture.
"I believe that all readers, whatever their different cultural experiences, will find in this novel something to identify with, and I hope that, through the personal accounts of the author, they will be able to trace the complex path which our nation travelled not so long ago." – Václav Havel
"Readers who enjoy good prose will find to their liking this imaginatively written and entertaining – but essentially tragic – novel set in the little-known 50s of the last century in Czechoslovakia." – Josef Škvorecký

FICTION – CHINESE LANGUAGE
THE MONKEY IN ME, by Caleb Kavon. Translated by Chapman Chen. May 2010. Ebook. 24Reader Ebook edition (2010) ISBN 9789881847997

TIGHTROPE! A BOHEMIAN TALE, by Olga Walló. Translated by Chapman Chen. Hong Kong. November 2011. pbk ISBN: 9789881993335

NON-FICTION

*CHOCOLATE'S BROWN STUDY IN THE BAG by Rupert Kwan Yun Chan. Hong Kong and the UK, March 2011. pbk. 112pp. plus 16 colour pp. illustrations. Proverse Prize Finalist (2009). ISBN: 978-988-19932-1-2.
http://www.chineseupress.com/asp/e_Book_card.asp?BookID=3054&Lang=E

"Rupert Chan has a light, humorous touch. Delightful. Witty". – Proverse Prize Judges, 2009.

*THE COMPLETE COURT CASES OF MAGISTRATE FREDERICK STEWART AS REPORTED IN *THE CHINA MAIL*, JULY 1881 TO MARCH 1882. Edited with commentary and chapters by Gillian Bickley. Indexed by Verner Bickley. Essay by Dr Ian Grant. Hong Kong and the UK, 2008. Preface by The Hon. Mr Justice Bokhary PJ, Court of Final Appeal. CD. 761pp. inc. notes, index. Supported by the Council of the Lord Wilson Heritage Trust.
ISBN-13: 978-988-17724-1-1.
www.chineseupress.com/asp/e_Book_card.asp?BookID=2559&Lang=E

"Together [these brief reports] do even more for the modern reader than put him in the armchair of someone who took the *China Mail* in Victorian Hong Kong – although that alone would be interesting enough. They provide him with a seat at the back of Mr Stewart's court, alive again and in session." – The Hon. Mr Justice Bokhary PJ.

CULTURAL RELATIONS IN THE GLOBAL COMMUNITY: PROBLEMS AND PROSPECTS. Edited by Verner Bickley and Puthenparampil John Philip. New Delhi, 1981. hbk. 255pp. ISBN-10: 81-7017-136-9; ISBN-13: 978-81-7017-136-2.

*THE DEVELOPMENT OF EDUCATION IN HONG KONG, 1841-1897: AS REVEALED BY THE EARLY EDUCATION REPORTS OF THE HONG KONG GOVERNMENT, 1848-1896. Ed. Gillian Bickley. Hong Kong and the United Kingdom, 2002. hbk. 633pp., inc. bibliography, index. The only collected, corrected, annotated, introduced, published edition of important source materials, with brief biographies of four of the writers *and archival photographs*. Supported by the Council of the Lord Wilson Heritage Trust.
ISBN-10: 962-85570-1-7; ISBN-13: 978-962-85570-1-1.
www.chineseupress.com/asp/e_Book_card.asp?BookID=1526&Lang=E
"An essential resource for those researching colonial education policy." – Norman Miners, University of Hong Kong, in, *The Journal of Imperial and Colonial History*.

FOCH'S RESERVES: THE CHINESE LABOUR CORPS (1917-1921), by Gregory James. Hong Kong and the UK, 2012. hbk. c. pp. 1,200 w. b/w illustrations. With "Roll of Honour" (q.v.) Proverse Prize Joint-Winner 2010. ISBN 9789881993427

FOOTFALLS ECHO IN THE MEMORY: A Life With The Colonial Education Service And The British Council In Asia, by Verner Bickley. London and New York, 2010. Forewords by Rt Hon the Lord Hunt of Wirral, MBE and Valerie Mitchell, OBE, Director-General, the English-Speaking Union of the Commonwealth. hbk. xviii+314pp. w. 20 b/w photographs. Supported by the Hong Kong Arts Development Council. ISBN: 978-1-84885-085-9. *Signed copies.*

Verner Bickley reviews his eventful life in a series of memory-filled footsteps. The memoirs of someone who has quietly experienced a very full life, continues to serve and continues to give through the telling of his story. – Valerie Pickard, HKADC Examiner

"A man's experience of a changing world." – Alice Tsay, *Asian Cha*, May 2010 (Issue 11).

*FORWARD TO BEIJING! A GUIDE TO THE SUMMER OLYMPICS, by Verner Bickley. Hong Kong and the UK, 29 February 2008. Message by Timothy Fok. Preface by the Hon. Dr. Arnaldo de Oliveira Sales. With an essay, "A Big Idea" by Chris Wardlaw.pbk. 260pp. w. 16 b/w photographs & author's portrait. ISBN-13: 978-988-99668-3-6.
www.chineseupress.com/asp/e_Book_card.asp?BookID=2318&Lang=E

"Explains for each Olympic Sport the rules, special terms & vocabulary. Lists impressive Olympiad achievements of the past. Contains fascinating insights into the history of the Games. Showcases the Beijing Olympics, the third Asian Summer Olympiad. Provides for visitors, & residents of Beijing & Hong Kong useful information, phrases, dialogues, quizzes and conversational openers."

"Comprehensive and scholarly. The idea is noble: encourage visitors to embrace the symbolic gesture of this third Asian summer Olympiad – international goodwill, cooperation and peace." – *Hong Kong Magazine.*

"Will appeal to the adult 'armchair enthusiast' seeking to get the most out of televised events. Appeals across age and gender, designed for longevity." – Vincent Heywood, *Chinese Cross Currents.*

*GIN'S TONIC: OCEAN VOYAGE, INNER JOURNEY, by Virginia MacRobert. Hong Kong and the UK, 2010. Preface by Ed Vaughan. pbk. 600pp., inc. index. Illustrations: colour photographs, author portrait. Supported by Hong Kong Arts Development Council. ISBN-13: 978-988-17724-3-5.
www.chineseupress.com/asp/e_Book_card.asp?BookID=2736&lang=E

Story of a journey round the world.

"What fun it will be to sail around the world with Ginni MacRobert as you read and ask yourself, 'what would I do now?!' It's an honour to welcome you aboard this book and to know that you are about to discover pure courage." – Ed Vaughan

"The book is soft and refreshing and tingles one's heart in such a way that your feelings go along with *Dai Long Wan*. A book to be read with profit." – Stephen Tang (Gu Song).

*THE GOLDEN NEEDLE: THE BIOGRAPHY OF FREDERICK STEWART (1836-1889), by Gillian Bickley. David C. Lam Institute for East-West Studies, Hong Kong Baptist University. Hong Kong and the UK, 1997. Foreword by Lady Saltoun. Introduction by Sir David Wilson (now Lord Wilson). pbk. 308pp., inc. bibliography, index. w. archival photographs. ISBN-10: 962-80270-8-5; ISBN-13: 978-962-8027-08-8.
www.chineseupress.com/asp/e_Book_card.asp?BookID=1550&Lang=E

The biography of the Founder of Hong Kong Government Education and first headmaster of Queen's College (then the Central School).

"Dr Bickley's life of Frederick Stewart is beautifully written, eminently readable, and at times moving." – Lady Saltoun.

"We need more studies of this type to understand fully the complexities of colonial rule." "[I] thoroughly enjoyed this book." – Clive Whitehead, University of Western Australia, *Int. J. of Lifelong Education.*

"Bickley tells the story with unswerving admiration and many vivid touches." – Douglas Hurd, *The Scotsman.*

*THE GOLDEN NEEDLE: THE BIOGRAPHY OF FREDERICK STEWART (1836-1889). <u>Full audio version</u> on 14 CDs. <u>Read by Verner Bickley</u>. ISRC HK-D94-00-00001-40.
www.chineseupress.com/asp/e_Book_card.asp?BookID=1552&Lang=E

<u>Also</u>, TEACHERS' AND STUDENTS' GUIDE TO THE BOOK AND AUDIO BOOK OF 'THE GOLDEN NEEDLE: THE BIOGRAPHY OF FREDERICK STEWART (1836-1889)'. Proverse Hong Kong Study Guides.

Mobipocket e-book. ISBN-10: 962-85570-9-2; ISBN-13: 978-962-85570-9-7.
24Reader Ebook edition (2010) ISBN 978-988-19320-5-1

*A MAGISTRATE'S COURT IN 19TH CENTURY HONG KONG: COURT IN TIME: Court Cases of The Honourable Frederick Stewart, MA, LLD, Founder of Hong Kong Government Education, Head of the Permanent HK Civil Service & Nineteenth Century HK Police Magistrate.

A Misted Mirror

Contributing Ed., Gillian Bickley. Contributors: Garry Tallentire, Geoffrey Roper, Timothy Hamlett, Christopher Coghlan, Verner Bickley. Preface by Sir T. L. Yang. Modern Commentary & Background Essays *with* Selected Themed Transcripts. 1st Edition. Hong Kong and the UK, 2005. pbk. 531pp. inc. bibliography, index, notes, w. 56 b/w archival illustrations. ISBN-10: 962-85570-4-1; ISBN-13: 978-962-85570-4-2.
www.chineseupress.com/asp/e_Book_card.asp?BookID=1898&Lang=E

"The contributors have written with insight and understanding ... a most readable book." – Sir T. L. Yang. "[The] lengthy introduction ... is a masterly and impartial survey." – Bradley Winterton, *Taipei Times.*

Mobibook e-book edition, 2005, revd 2008 with the new title: A Magistrate's Court in Nineteenth Century Hong Kong: Court in Time: the Court Cases Reported in *The China Mail* of The Honourable Frederick Stewart, MA, LLD, Founder of Hong Kong Government Education, Head of the Permanent Hong Kong Civil Service & Nineteenth Century Hong Kong Police Magistrate. Modern Commentary & Background Essays with Selected Themed Transcripts and Modern Photographs of Heritage Buildings of the Magistracy, Prison and Court of Final Appeal. ISBN-10: 962-85570-7-6; ISBN-13: 978-962-85570-7-3.

*A MAGISTRATE'S COURT IN 19TH CENTURY HONG KONG With additional discussion of "The Opium Ordinance": COURT IN TIME: 2nd ed. Hong Kong and the UK, 2009. pbk. 536pp. inc. bibliography, index, notes, w. 56 b/w archival illustrations. ISBN-13: 978-962-17724-5-9.
www.chineseupress.com/asp/e_Book_card.asp?BookID=2559&Lang=E

MEMOIRS OF AN ICE-CREAM LADY by Emily Ho. Hong Kong and the UK, November 2011. pbk. 4C Cartoons by Emily Ho. 4C Photographs.
Proverse Prize Publication Prize 2010. ISBN-13: 978-988-19933-0-4.

A charming and humorous series of anecdotes by a Chinese lady, mostly related to her establishing and managing an ice-cream shop on the Hong Kong island of Lamma.

"A story of love and betrayal, told simply and straight from the heart. This charming story of an ice-cream parlor in Hong Kong's Lamma Island is a whimsical mixture of crazy characters, wise sayings, anecdotes, history and fantasies." — Patricia W. Grey, Author of *Death Has A Thousand Doors*

*A PERSONAL JOURNEY THROUGH SKETCHING: THE SKETCHER'S ART, by Errol Patrick Hugh. Hong Kong and the UK, 2009. Introduction by Li Shiqiao. hbk. 96pp. with 100+ original sketches and photographs by the author & author's portrait. 300mm x 215mm x 14mm. w. CD-ROM. ISBN-13: 978-988-18479-1-1.
www.chineseupress.com/asp/e_Book_card.asp?BookID=2657&Lang=E

Aims to highlight the artistic energies and the practical wisdom behind the process of the art of sketching, so that readers see the simplicity and magic of complex, on-site, hand-drawn sketches.

"Each sketch is invested with a narrative that links to acts of observation and documentation through engaging afresh with our primary senses. Errol has never lost sight of the fundamental importance of sketching. I take great comfort in seeing the nimble and discerning connections between the eye and the hand in Errol's elegant lines and considered compositions." – Li Shiqiao.

ROLL OF HONOUR, by Gregory James. Hong Kong and the UK. CD. Photographs, including archival photographs. With "Foch's Reserves" (q.v.), Proverse Prize Joint-Winner 2010. ISBN 9789881993434

SEARCHING FOR FREDERICK AND ADVENTURES ALONG THE WAY, by Verner Bickley. Hong Kong, 2001. pbk. 420pp., inc. bibliography, index. w. author's portrait. *With archival and modern photographs.* Supported by the Hong Kong Arts Development Council. ISBN-10:962-8783-20-3; ISBN-13:978-962-8783-20-5.

The story of the book, *The Golden Needle* (the biography of the Founder of Hong Kong Government Education). Narrative of research, with anecdotes, useful addresses and contact information, intermixed with stories and reflections from the author's own life experience, mainly in Asia.

"Verner Bickley writes in a mostly light-hearted vein, with a gentle humour." – Sir James Hodge, British Consul General, Hong Kong.

SEMPER FI: THE STORY OF A VIETNAM ERA MARINE, by Orville Leverne Clubb. Hong Kong and the UK, 2012. pbk. Illustrations: photographs, sketch-maps. ISBN 13: 978-988-19933-4-2.

SEMPER FI gives a portrait of a young man and his experiences as an enlisted member of the US Marine Corps during the Vietnam War. Orville Clubb begins at the beginning with his earliest memories and tells the story right through to his discharge after serving overseas. Born into a poor family brought together by World War II, the writer grew to maturity as a young Marine. As with many young men of this era of similar socio-economic status, joining the military as an enlisted man was an attractive option that offered a new start of life. ISBN: 9789881993342

*SPANKING GOALS AND TOE POKES: FOOTBALL SAYINGS EXPLAINED, by T. J. Martin. Hong Kong and the UK, June 2008. Edited by Gillian Bickley. Indexed by Verner Bickley. Preface by John Dykes. pbk. 106pp. w. 16 b/w illustrations by Jacinta Read & two author's portraits (one with Sir Stanley Matthews). ISBN-13: 978-988-99668-2-9. www.chineseupress.com/asp/e_Book_card.asp?BookID=2451&Lang=E

Lists and explains more than 800 of the sayings that football commentators use. An enjoyable reference tool which can increase readers' understanding of English language football commentaries and colloquial English expressions in general.

"Entertaining. – We have all heard these sayings but now we have easy explanations and some very funny illustrations to call on. A must read football book for fans everywhere." – Paul Truman, Mobipocket website, June 2008.

*THE STEWARTS OF BOURTREEBUSH. Aberdeen, UK, Centre for Scottish Studies, University of Aberdeen, 2003. pbk. 153pp. Extensive documentation of the Scottish family of the Founder of Hong Kong Government Education, Frederick Stewart presenting the perspective of each family member. As such, a reference to writing family history and biography. *With archival photographs and facsimiles of documents, Hong Kong & Scottish subjects.* ISBN-10: 0906265347; ISBN-13: 978-0-906265-34-5.
www.chineseupress.com/asp/e_Book_card.asp?BookID=1787&Lang=E

In a follow-up to her biography of renowned Hong Kong educationalist Frederick Stewart, Dr Gillian Bickley turns the spotlight on his Aberdeenshire, Scotland family. Her archival search, often with her husband Dr Verner Bickley, serves as a model for other researchers engaged in family history.

*WANNABE BACKPACKERS: THE LATIN AMERICAN & KENYAN JOURNEY OF FIVE SPOILED TEENAGERS by Gerald Yeung. Hong Kong and the UK, 11 March 2009. pbk. 164pp. (w. several b/w pix). ISBN 978-988-17724-2-8.
http://www.chineseupress.com/asp/e_Book_card.asp?BookID=2522&Lang=E

The story of five self-confessed "spoiled teenagers" who travel to Latin America and Kenya one summer.

"A Hong Kong story of roughing it the nice way. The story is about the interaction among the five during their 30 days on the road together. 'Some things we found out about each other, we really didn't want to know.'" – Annemarie Evans, *South China Morning Post*.

"Written in diary style, the book conveys the precarious state of a young man poised between a protected childhood and imminent independence as an adult, providing fabulous insight for parents into what's really going on in a teen's mind. Encounters with girls, 'weird' food and clubbing in a foreign language are balanced with budding understanding of the differences of other cultures and appreciation of their beauty. Each of the friends adds their own epilogue summing up the group's collective experience." – *Parents' Journal*, Hong Kong.

NON-FICTION – CHINESE LANGUAGE
THE GOLDEN NEEDLE: THE BIOGRAPHY OF FREDERICK STEWART (1836-1889): SELECTIONS, by Gillian Bickley. Translated by Hong-Lok Kwok. May 2010, E-bk. ISBN: 978988189050402

POETRY
ASTRA AND SEBASTIAN: An Epic Love Story by L.W. Illsley. Hong Kong and the UK, November 2011. pbk. Illustrated by Shelley Knowles-Dixon. Proverse Prize Finalist 2010. ISBN: 978-988-19932-4-3.

Illsley's *Astra and Sebastian* is a poetic saga that strives towards timeless spectacle, through a textual feast for the senses. This is imaginative, phantasmagoric verse on a grand scale; in which heroic myth, punctuated by motifs of the dream-work and the unconscious, draws the reader into the human quest for love, self-knowledge, adventure and transcendence. – Mary-Jane Newton, author of the poetry collection, *Of Symbols Misused*

*CHINA SUITE AND OTHER POEMS by Gillian Bickley. Hong Kong and the UK, November 2009. Preface by Elbert S. P. Lee. Recommendation by Karmel Schreyer. Supported by the Hong Kong Arts Development Council. pbk. 136pp. w. 2 no. audio CDs. ISBN-13: 978-988-17724-9-7. www.chineseupress.com/asp/e_Book_card.asp?BookID=2658&Lang=E

"The poems in *China Suite* are unpretentious, direct, and even raw, like gemstones freshly dug out of a quarry. The psychological boundaries drawn to separate cultures from cultures, clans from clans, and individual from individual are utterly destroyed." – Elbert S. P. Lee

"A collection refined by the sensitivity and spirit of a poet who observes with the wonder and clarity of someone who is at once an insider and outsider. In her works, we see that Bickley's poetry has the ability to provide both spontaneous, on-the-spot immediacy and lingering, contemplative power...." – Hilary Chan Tsz-Shan, *Asian Cha*, February 2010 (Issue 10).

*FOR THE RECORD AND OTHER POEMS OF HONG KONG, by Gillian Bickley. Hong Kong and the UK, 2003. Preface by Rosanna Wong. pbk. 118pp. w. author's portrait. Sixty poems written during a residence of 30 years in Hong Kong. With a talk given to the English Society of the University of Hong Kong. With two CDs of all poems read by the author. Supported by the Hong Kong Arts Development Council.
ISBN-10: 962-85570-2-5; ISBN-13: 978-962-85570-2-8.
www.chineseupress.com/asp/e_Book_card.asp?BookID=1732&Lang=E

People, nature, city-scenes, thoughts, experiences, cultural performances.
"Thought-provoking and entertaining." – David Wilson, *Sunday Morning Post*, Hong Kong.

*HEART TO HEART, by Patty Ho. Hong Kong and the UK, 2010. Illustrations by the writer's sister, Annie Ho. Preface by Winston Ka-Sun Chu. pbk. 104pp. Supported by the Hong Kong Arts Development Council. ISBN 978-988-17724-0-4.
www.chineseupress.com/asp/e_Book_card.asp?BookID=2738&lang=E

"A remarkably engaging and edifying book of simple but thought-provoking poems, [a] timely reminder to the reading public that Hong Kong has more to offer than the sum of its literary, cultural and political stereotypes. If the concept of 'one world' is worth anything in this postmodern age of globalist cynicism, Patty Ho's poetry causes us to reflect on what is quintessentially human and on the fragile beauty of all existence." – Mike Ingham
– "Along with the carefully chosen photographs and thought-provoking watercolour illustrations provided by Ho's sister, the collection constitutes a dynamic conversation between visual and written texts about the emotions and values we all share." – Flora Mak, in *Cha: An Asian literary Journal*, Issue 12, September 2010.

HOME, AWAY, ELSEWHERE by Vaughan Rapatahana. Hong Kong and the UK, November 2011. Preface by James Norcliffe. pbk. 208pp. Proverse Prize Semi-Finalist 2009. ISBN 13: 978-988-19932-2-9.

"Vaughan Rapataha's poems make significant patterns out of the randomness of life's events and give succinct and effective voice to the peculiarly modern condition of the global nomad at once home everywhere and home nowhere." – David Eggleton, Editor of *Landfall*, Aotearoa-New Zealand.

*IMMORTELLE AND BHANDAARAA POEMS by Lelawattee Manoo-Rahming. Hong Kong and the UK, 9 March 2011. Preface by Sandra Pouchet Paquet, PhD, Professor Emerita of English, University of Miami. pbk. 176pp. (plus 8 colour pp. w. 9 original pieces of artwork by the author.) Proverse Prize Finalist 2009. ISBN 978-988-19321-3-6.
http://www.chineseupress.com/asp/e_Book_card.asp?BookID=3052&Lang=E

Inspired by the Hindu philosophy of reincarnation, many of the poems are written in memory of loved ones, filled with scenes from the poet's physical landscape which spans the Caribbean, from The Bahamas, her present home, to Trinidad, the land of her birth. The language of these sensual poems is a syncretism of the poet's East Indian-derived Bhojpuri Hindi and her Trinbagonian creole, peppered with nuances of the Bahamian vernacular. This syncretism is reflected in the themes of the poems. Although many of the poems deal with Indo-Caribbean anthropology, the collection embraces other cultures and religions which are present in the Caribbean, and speaks to the fluidity in philosophy that can exist and flourish, in such plural societies. *Immortelle and Bhandaaraa Poems* is a celebration of life and a testament to the lives of those who have passed on.
"Lelawattee Manoo-Rahming is a poet and mixed media artist of great range and complexity; all of the world and its myriad experiences are her concern. These collected works range in both content and tone from the sacred to the profane, from grief to joy, and the journey both in its language and vision is impressive and courageous. Manoo-Rahming guides the reader through national, regional, and familial history while simultaneously revealing, mourning and celebrating her diverse cultural inheritance." – Sandra Pouchet Paquet, Ph.D., Professor Emerita of English, University of Miami.

*MOVING HOUSE AND OTHER POEMS FROM HONG KONG, by Gillian Bickley. With a talk given in the English Department Staff Seminar Series at Hong Kong Baptist University. Hong Kong and the UK, 2005. Preface by Chung Ling. pbk. 130pp. w. author's portrait. With one CD of all poems read by the author.
ISBN-10:962-85570-5-X; ISBN-13: 978-962-85570-5-9.
www.chineseupress.com/asp/e_Book_card.asp?BookID=1992&Lang=E

"The variety of human life and the individual response to life, these are Gillian Bickley's central interests." – Emeritus Professor I. F. Clarke and M. Clarke, UK.

*OF SYMBOLS MISUSED by Mary-Jane Newton. Foreword by Peter Carpenter. pbk. 96pp. ISBN: 978-988-19321-5-0.
http://www.chineseupress.com/asp/e_Book_card.asp?BookID=3051&Lang=E

A Misted Mirror

"Mary-Jane Newton's first collection displays boldness of spirit and a buccaneering sense of adventure in its forays with language, matched by energy, a wry sense of humour and humility in the light of the poet's responsibilities, thus making it a joy to read, at turns sensuous and arch in tones and angles."
– Peter Carpenter, author of *After the Goldrush* and Chair of the Poetry Society UK.
*PAINTING THE BORROWED HOUSE: POEMS, by Kate Rogers. Hong Kong and the UK, March 2008. Preface by Donna Langevin. pbk. 68pp. w. 3 b/w photographs & author's portrait. Supported by the Hong Kong Arts Development Council. ISBN-13: 978-988-99668-4-3. www.chineseupress.com/asp/e_Book_card.asp?BookID=2363&Lang=E

Kate Rogers's first book of poetry. An honest, fresh account by a complex and sensitive woman who has travelled from her native Canada to see and experience new places, people and cultures. – This collection follows her journey as she explores Asia, her life changes and she finally commits herself to remain, learning to live with her choices in a new culture, the "Borrowed House" of the title.

Kate sees beyond the usual dimensions of every day and is open to strange and novel experiences. She reaches out to us through these poems and creates gentle and poignant bonds with her readers. Her perceptions encourage us to be conscious of the archaeology and layered structure of our own lives.

Full of epiphanies, vivid emotion and surprise.

"Ostensibly a voyage through China, Hong Kong and Taiwan, it is really a journey through the emotions." – Bill Purves, author of *China on the Lam*.

"Here is an author in her prime; confident, sure of her craft, and willing to take risks." – Donna Langevin, author of *Improvising in the Dark* and *The Second Language of Birds*.

"These are the poems of a restless muse, sifting and searching a spiritual identity in a foreign land. The Borrowed House is a metaphor with undertones of synecdoche to express the pull and disorientation of the expat with a lust for wandering far from home. . .. I found myself warming and responding to these poems. . . . there are some very alluring verbal pictures and she is particularly focused on endings that linger in the mind." – Paul Bench, *Word Matters*, Journal of the Society of Teachers of Speech and Drama, Summer 2009, Vol. 59, No. 1, p. 45.

POEMS TO ENJOY (w. sound recording of all poems). Verner Bickley, editor & anthologiser. Hong Kong Educational Publishing Co. pbk. 3 vols of graded poetry anthologies (kindergarten to adult), with Teachers' Notes. ISBN-10: 962-290-018-6; ISBN-13: 978-962-290-018-9; ISBN-10: 962-290-019-4; ISBN-13: 978-962-290-019-6; ISBN-10: 962-290-020-8; ISBN-13: 978-962-290-020-2.

REFRAIN, by Jason S. Polley. Hong Kong and the UK, 23 November 2010. Preface by Kirby Wright. pbk. 88pp. Entered for the inaugural Proverse Prize (2009). ISBN: 978-988-19321-4-3. www.chineseupress.com/asp/e_Book_card.asp?BookID=2944 &Lang=E

refrain recounts the author's travels in India as an inexperienced and sensitive young man. The narrative shows wit, intelligence and a facility with words. The style is experimental and literary; and the fascination of the stories told – short stories in verse presenting the anxieties and misfortunes typical of shoestring traveling, and the culture-shock deriving from visiting a very different culture from ones own – carries the careful reader along. A knack for reading this less-than-conventional fast-paced book, which is at once humorous and nightmarish, passionate and detached, is acquired quickly.

"A young man arrives in Delhi with a romanticized view of India, a pocketful of outdated maps, and a money belt begging to be stolen. We experience his battles with disgust and paranoia while moving through a rough and tumble city. Polley takes us along on a ride that feels cinematic, jammed with sensory explosions that rock the sensibilities. The reader is pulled into the text to experience the chaotic, disordered images of India. Polley paints on a large canvas and his brush strokes are fresh, memorable, and cutting edge. – Kirby Wright, Honolulu, Hawaii, Author of *Punahou Blues* and *Moloka'i Nui Ahina*

*SIGHTINGS: A COLLECTION OF POETRY, WITH AN ESSAY, "COMMUNICATING POEMS", by Gillian Bickley. With a talk given in the English Department Staff Seminar Series at Hong Kong Baptist University. Hong Kong and the UK, 2007. Introduction by Ma Kwai Hung. Preface by Harry Guest. Foreword by Marion Bethel. pbk. 142pp. w. author's portrait. Supported by the Hong Kong Arts Development Council. ISBN-13: 978-988-99668-1-2.
www.chineseupress.com/asp/e_Book_card.asp?BookID=2264&Lang=E
"Bickley has made use of everyday life situations and turned them into life lessons. *Sightings* inspires us to slow down and taste the sense of the city." – Ma Kwai Hung, Examiner, Hong Kong Arts Development Council.

SMOKED PEARL: Poems of Hong Kong and Beyond, by Akin Jeje (Akinsola Olufemi Jeje). Hong Kong and the UK, 23 November 2010. Preface by Viki Holmes. pbk. 132pp. Supported by the Hong Kong Arts Development Council. Proverse Prize Semi-finalist (2009). ISBN 978-988-19321-1-2.
www.chineseupress.com/asp/e_Book_card.asp?BookID=2943&Lang=E

Chronicles observations and experiences in Hong Kong, Canada and Africa.
"A fine collection of free verse; exuberant and thoughtful. Serious, thoughtful and moral; angry, but also loving and compassionate." – Proverse Prize Judges.
"Jeje sees the gleam revealed within the grime: his titular smoked pearl evocative of this interplay of light and dark. For tarnished things must once have been precious, and though Jeje writes of wasted days, he recognises the briefness, 'the glory of the blaze.' ... But for all that Jeje sees – the injustice, the silence and the blame – these darknesses of the human soul are not total: the night ends, hope dawns." – Viki Holmes, author of *miss moon's class*.
"Jeje's gaze swivels from the intensely private to the trans-continentally public, but he remains ever a self-confessed "jack swinger of verbs," offering us luscious, "amorous nouns." Lustillusion. Despairconfusion. This profusion of sights and sounds is tender, scintillating, thought provoking. Priceless." – Xu Xi, author of *Habit of a Foreign Sky* and *Evanescent Isles*.

WONDER, LUST & ITCHY FEET by Sally Dellow. Hong Kong and the UK, November 2011. Preface: David McKirdy. pbk. 176pp. Proverse Prize Publication Prize 2010.
ISBN 13: 978-988-19932-7-4.
A fearless, intelligent and eager woman—mother, lover, wife and daughter—collects for the first time a selection of poetry from her first four decades of living and writing. Unhesitatingly she exposes intimate feelings and heartfelt values about friendship, family, desire, disaster, finding a home and exploring the world.
"Wonder, Lust & Itchy Feet is an intimate journey; the emotional vulnerability gives the pieces their veracity. Tellingly, many Hong Kong poems in the Itchy Feet section declare an unavowed commitment to the place that she has made her home. Perhaps she has scratched that particular itch for the last time. – David McKirdy, author of *Accidental Oriental*.

POETRY– CHINESE LANGUAGE
FOR THE RECORD AND OTHER POEMS OF HONG KONG, by Gillian Bickley. Translated by Simon Chow. Hong Kong, May 2010. E-bk. ISBN: 9789881890559

*MOVING HOUSE AND OTHER POEMS FROM HONG KONG, TRANSLATED INTO CHINESE, WITH ADDITIONAL MATERIAL, by Gillian Bickley. Edited by Tony Ming-Tak YIP. Translated by Tony Yip & others. Hong Kong and the UK, June 2008. pbk. 140pp. w. nine b/w photographs & editor's portrait. ISBN-13: 962988996680.
www.chineseupress.com/asp/e_Book_card.asp?BookID=2452&lang=C